1999–2000 Annual Supplement to

THE PIANO BOOK

BUYING & OWNING A NEW OR USED PIANO

LARRY FINE

BROOKSIDE PRESS • BOSTON, MASSACHUSETTS

Brookside Press
P.O. Box 178, Jamaica Plain, Massachusetts 02130
(617) 522-7182
(800) 888-4741 (orders)

pianobk@tiac.net
www.tiac.net/users/pianobk

ISBN 1-929145-00-4

NOTICE

Reasonable efforts have been made to secure accurate information for this publication. Due in part to the fact that manufacturers and distributors will not always willingly make this information available, however, some indirect sources have been relied upon.

Neither the author nor publisher make any guarantees with respect to the accuracy of the information contained herein and will not be liable for damages—incidental, consequential, or otherwise—resulting from the use of the information.

INTRODUCTION

Given the long time span between new editions of *The Piano Book,* it's impractical to provide in the book itself the detailed model and price data that piano shoppers increasingly seek. Similarly, updated information about manufacturers and products is needed in a timely manner. This *Annual Supplement to The Piano Book*, published each August, is designed to fill that information gap. I hope this modest companion volume will effectively extend the "shelf life" of *The Piano Book* as a valuable reference work, and serve as an additional information resource for piano buyers and piano lovers.

Larry Fine

June, 1999

CONTENTS

MANUFACTURER and PRODUCT UPDATE

This section describes changes to companies, products, and brand names since the third edition of *The Piano Book* went to press in late 1994. The listings are cumulative; that is, where still relevant, information contained in last year's *Supplement* has been retained, and changes that have occurred during the past year have been added. If a company or brand name is not listed here, it means that there is nothing new of substance to report.

It is not intended, of course, that the information in this update section take the place of the reviews in *The Piano Book*. With some exceptions, the update is limited to changes of a factual nature only, whereas the book contains, in addition, critical reviews and recommendations. Readers should understand that, in most cases, changes in the quality of any particular brand of piano occur very slowly, over a period of many years, if at all. Only where there has been an abrupt change in company ownership, or a period of rapid technological or economic change in the country of origin, is there likely to be a change in quality worth worrying about. For that reason, the reviews in *The Piano Book*, though dated in some respects, can still be considered reliable unless otherwise noted here.

The Global Piano Market—An Update

The past two years have seen Chinese and Indonesian pianos join the mainstream piano community for the first time. Several years of investment in infrastructure and training by piano manufacturers in joint venture with the Chinese government, and in Indonesia, have just started to bear fruit. Prior to two years ago, many pianos from this part of the world had too many obvious gross defects to be taken seriously. Most of the new manufacturing capacity in China is devoted to the market created by the rapidly growing Chinese middle class. A smaller portion is being diverted to the U.S. and other markets, aimed at consumers who would otherwise purchase an inexpensive used piano.

For some, these new Chinese and Indonesian pianos may indeed be a viable alternative to a used one, especially in areas where good used pianos are hard to come by or when shopping time is limited. But while many of these instruments are now acceptable, the quality is far from uniform or consistent, and the majority require extensive adjusting by the importer or dealer. Prospective customers should be reminded that these are, at best, entry-level pianos and that they have little or no track record. In addition, brand names and distributorships are in flux as the players position themselves in the market, so some warranties may offer less security than others. I would recommend, therefore, for the time being, that purchase be limited to those brands whose warranties are backed by major manufacturers or distributors. Additionally, a warranty from the dealer might be advisable.

Of course, Chinese and Indonesian pianos are attractive primarily because of their low price. Some of the wind was taken out of this "Chinese miracle" last year by the devaluation of the Korean currency and the subsequent drop in price of Korean pianos by ten to twenty-five percent. Now quite satisfactory for the entry-level and mid-level piano buyer, Korean instruments are an especially good value for the money at this time. Due to low labor costs and other favorable conditions, some Eastern European pianos are also a good value in mid-level instruments, with particularly pleasing tonal qualities, but require diligent preparation by the dealer to realize their potential.

As always, Japanese pianos are fine for the mid-level (and slightly higher) piano buyer, especially for those whose requirements are fairly generic in nature and are looking for a quick, dependable, "off-the-shelf" solution to a piano need. However, the gap in price between Japanese pianos and their Korean competitors has widened, making the former a little less attractive. For the upper-level piano buyer looking for performance more than value, there continues to be an excellent selection of instruments from Western Europe and the United States to satisfy every taste.

The market for electronic player pianos and hybrid digital/acoustic pianos has intensified. Two companies, Yamaha and Baldwin, feature player piano systems that are available only on their own pianos; two others, PianoDisc and QRS, make systems that can be installed into any piano. In comparing these systems, there is no substitute for listening. I suspect, though, that most casual users of the playback systems will be able to discern little difference between them. Special attention should be paid, however, to the library of music available for them and to what extent they are compatible with the music of other systems. There is a growing trend toward compatibility, but the details are sometimes vague. For sophisticated recording and composing, the differences between the systems may be more substantial. Musicians who plan to use these systems for those purposes should examine the features in more depth than can be covered here.

August Förster—See "Förster, August"

Baldorr & Son—Name discontinued

Baldwin

New corporate address and phone:

Baldwin Piano & Organ Co.
4680 Parkway Drive
Mason, Ohio 45040

513-754-4500

At the time the third edition of *The Piano Book* was going to press, Baldwin was in the process of completely reorganizing its product line (and also undergoing major changes in management). The description of the new models given in the book was based on Baldwin's tentative plans at that time, but the plans changed and the actual product line turned out a little differently.

Baldwin also owns the **Wurlitzer** and **Chickering** trade names. In its reorganized product line, the Wurlitzers represent the lower-priced pianos, the Chickerings the mid-priced American-made grands, and the Baldwins the mid- to upper-level verticals and high-end grands. All are sold by the same dealer network. (In the past, Wurlitzer and Baldwin/Chickering had separate dealer networks, and the Baldwin line included instruments at all price levels, which tended to confuse customers about the relative value of the Baldwin name.)

In the new Baldwin line, the spinet model has been discontinued. The console, 43-1/2" in height, comes in three basic model types. The three differ in cabinetry, but use the same back and action, including Baldwin's 19-ply hard rock maple pinblock, a solid spruce soundboard, and a "Full Blow" (full-size, direct blow) action. (All Baldwin verticals now have these features.) The model E100 is the console with a continental-style cabinet. It has a slightly longer key length and deeper cabinet than the continental-style model it replaces. The model 660 series console is a furniture-style model known as the "Classic." The upper-level console, the model 2090 series, is called the "Acrosonic," a name Baldwin has traditionally used for its upper-level consoles and spinets. This model series has fancier cabinet features and hardware than the Classic, but is the same instrument inside.

Baldwin 45" studio verticals, still known as the "Hamilton," come in three model types. The model 243HPA is the school studio. Its functional-looking cabinet has been redesigned to provide easier access for servicing, as well as for other practical reasons. The model 5050 series studio, known as the "Limited Edition," is the fancy-looking studio. It is made in only three furniture styles, each limited to a production run of one thousand instruments, after which the style is changed. The model E250 is the studio in a contemporary cabinet style. The model 248, a 48" "Professional Upright," introduced in 1997, contains many interesting new technical features aimed primarily at enhancing tuning stability and evenness of tone. The model 6000 52" "Concert Vertical" upright remains the same.

The Baldwin "Artist" series of grand pianos has undergone the following changes: All Baldwin Artist grands are now being shipped with Renner hammers, and the weight characteristics of the action have been changed to reduce inertia; each piano now comes with an adjustable Artist bench; the sharps are now made of solid ebony wood instead of plastic; and a 5' 8" Louis XVI style (model 227) has been added to the line. During the past few years, Baldwin has invested heavily in new computer-controlled woodworking machinery for greater precision in manufacturing lids and other parts, and in new polyester finishing equipment. All high-gloss finishes for Baldwin Artist grands are now produced in polyester.

The Chickering line of American-made grands is new. The two models, 4' 10" (model 410) and 5' 7" (model 507), are adapted from the Classic line of Baldwin grands that was discontinued at the end of 1994. According to Baldwin, the new models have been redesigned and structurally enhanced. In 1998, several period-style furniture models were added to the Chickering line.

The Wurlitzer vertical piano line is now limited to a 37" spinet with a full-size but indirect-blow action, and an entry-level 42" console with a compressed, direct-blow action. Baldwin's Kranich & Bach line of Chinese-made pianos has been discontinued, but the 42" console from that line is now offered with the Wurlitzer name on it (model WP50), in addition to the American-made 42" Wurlitzer console (model 2270 series). All other Wurlitzer consoles, studios, and uprights, both American-made and Korean-made, have been discontinued, as have the Wurlitzer 5' grand (model G550) and all Wurlitzer grands made by Young Chang. All grands with the Wurlitzer name are now made by Samick (4' 7", 5' 1", and 5' 8") and are the same as the grands formerly bearing the name "D.H. Baldwin," a name which is no longer being used.

Baldwin's ConcertMaster electronic player piano system was introduced in 1997. ConcertMaster can be factory-installed or field-installed (retrofitted) into virtually any model of Baldwin, Wurlitzer, or Chickering piano, including verticals. ConcertMaster utilizes playback solenoid technology from QRS that is customized for Baldwin products, including a low-profile solenoid rail design on factory-installed systems. ConcertMaster comes with a floppy disk drive, a compact disc (CD) drive, and a 1.2-gigabyte hard drive—a three-playback-source design exclusive to Baldwin—pre-loaded with 20 hours of music. Baldwin says the floppy disk drive can read just about any type of General MIDI music software on the market, including such software made for other systems, and the CD drive can read the QRS CDs containing analog audio accompaniment. The hard drive has a capacity of 10,000 songs, which can be input from any MIDI source, including computer disks, the internet, and so forth. ConcertMaster now can read video discs, too, allowing you to view on your television set multi-media software performances of Baldwin artists performing "live" while your piano plays every note the artist does. (ConcertMaster was named the "Best New Product Technology" in 1998 by the Custom Electronic Design and Installation Association due to its ability to be integrated into whole-house audio and video systems.)

ConcertMaster's operating system is software upgradeable, allowing new features to be added without purchasing new hardware. A "Performance option" adds recording capabilities and turns the piano into a MIDI controller, complete with velocity sensitivity, assignable split point, and other features. An optional hammer stop rail is available to silence the piano, allowing you to listen via headphones to the hundreds of voices that can be accessed, or to play them through the speakers that come with the system. ConcertMaster can be operated via a stationary controller attached under the front or side of the piano or by a 900 MHz hand-held radio-frequency remote control with 100-plus channels and a built-in LCD window, included.

Bechner—Name discontinued

Becker, J.—Distribution discontinued.

Belarus—Name discontinued. See "Schubert"

Bentley—See "Whelpdale Maxwell & Codd"

Bergmann—See "Young Chang"

Betting, Th.—Name discontinued. See "Schirmer & Son"

Blondel, G. (new listing)

A-440 Pianos
4100 Steve Reynolds Blvd., Suite F
Norcross, Georgia 30093

770-717-8047
888-565-5648

Georges Blondel was a French piano technician who worked for many years for the former Belgian piano manufacturer A. Hanlet. Now located in Paris, Pianos Hanlet S.A. is the largest piano dealer and distributor in France. After Blondel's death, Hanlet commemorated his years of service by using his name on a line of pianos distributed throughout Europe. The pianos are manufactured for Hanlet by the Bohemia Piano Co., makers of Rieger-Kloss pianos, in the Czech Republic, and are similar to the Rieger-Kloss models of similar size. All models have Renner actions, Delignit pinblocks, and agraffes throughout the scale.

Blüthner

A new "Haessler" line of pianos has been added to the Blüthner product line. (Haessler is a Blüthner family name.) Created to compete better in the American market, Haessler pianos have more conventional technical and cosmetic features than the regular models and cost about twenty-five percent less. For example, the grands are loop-strung instead of single-strung; omit the "aliquot" strings (fourth string per note); and have normal, straight-cut, angle-mounted hammers. Case and plate cosmetics are simpler. The Haessler line now contains several vertical models and 5' 8" and 6' 1" grands. For prices, see under "Haessler" in the Pricing Guide section of this *Supplement*.

Bohemia / Rieger-Kloss

New importer/distributor:

Weber Piano Co.
40 Seaview Drive
Secaucus, New Jersey 07094

800-346-5351
201-902-0920

The Czech company that makes Rieger-Kloss pianos has changed its name from "IFM Piana" to "Bohemia Piano Co." At present, the Bohemia name is used only on the 7' and 9' grands, Rieger-Kloss on all other models.

The Bohemia and Rieger-Kloss grands utilize cases and plates (strung backs) made in Korea by Young Chang, identical to those of similarly sized Young Chang models. The actions are made in Germany by Renner, the hammers are by Abel, and everything else is made in the Czech Republic, where the components are assembled. Rieger-Kloss verticals still use mostly Czech components, except for the 50" upright model R-125, which has a Renner action. Note that the 44" model R-111 is less expensive because the cabinet is finished in a photo finish that simulates a wood finish without using actual wood veneers.

Bösendorfer

New U.S. distributor address and phone:

Bösendorfer Pianos
8331 W. State Rd. #56
West Baden Springs, Indiana 47469

888-936-2516
812-936-4522

As reported in *The Piano Book*, the 7' Bösendorfer model 213 was introduced in 1990 to compete in the American market with the Steinway model B. It had, among other features, duplex scaling and 92 notes. In 1998, the model 213 was replaced by the 7' model 214. The new model, now without duplex scaling, is more traditional and consistent with the rest of the Bösendorfer line in its design. It also has only 88 notes.

In other changes, Bösendorfer has switched from leather key bushings to cloth, and the SE Reproducing System has been discontinued.

Bösendorfer is still owned by Kimball International, even though Kimball no longer manufactures pianos (see "Kimball").

Boston

A 5' 1" grand has been added to the line.

Broadwood, John, & Sons—See "Whelpdale Maxwell & Codd"

Chickering—See "Baldwin"

Disklavier—See "Yamaha"

Dobbert, Fritz (new listing)

These pianos are manufactured in Brazil and made their debut in the U.S. a few years ago. However, distribution in the U.S. has been discontinued.

Estonia

New toll-free phone number: 888-4 ESTONIA (437-8664)

5' 4" and 5' 6" grand models have been added to the line. Renner action and Abel hammers are now standard on all models.

The review of Estonia pianos in the third edition of *The Piano Book* was based on very limited information. Since then, the company has made improvements to the pianos and they have received positive reviews from many musicians. Although long-term service information is not yet available, no significant problems have been reported to me, and the Estonia pianos I have played have sounded quite good. Among the changes introduced in 1999 are new action geometry, a new pedal mechanism, and a new duplex scale on the 6' 3" model. Some of the models are now also available in exotic wood finishes.

Correction to historical information: The Tallinn Piano Factory (now Estonia Piano Factory) was founded in 1893 by Ernst Hiis under his own name. Around 1950, the government of Estonia consolidated many smaller Estonian piano makers into the Hiis factory under the Tallinn name. This factory focuses primarily on making grand pianos and says that it is the largest maker of grands among Scandinavian countries and Eastern Europe.

Eterna—See "Yamaha"

Everett

Wrightwood Enterprises, Inc.
717 St. Joseph Drive
St. Joseph, Michigan 49085

773-508-6615

The Everett name has been used on pianos by Wrightwood Enterprises, Inc. since 1995. Wrightwood's current Everett pianos are imported from, and made by, Dongbei Piano Manufactory in China. Prior to 1990, the Everett name had been used by Yamaha on various U.S.-made pianos. Yamaha discontinued its Everett piano brand in 1989.

Falcone—See "Mason & Hamlin"

Fandrich—Out of production

Fandrich & Sons (new listing)

Fandrich & Sons Pianos
12515 Lake City Way, NE
Seattle, Washington 98125

206-361-1221
888-460-9198

Fandrich & Sons pianos are sold by the people who invented the Fandrich Vertical Action™. The vertical pianos are made in China by the Guangzhou Piano Manufactory, the same company that makes Pearl River pianos. (A new 49" vertical is a joint venture between Yamaha and Guangzhou.) Fandrich & Sons makes extensive modifications and improvements to the pianos in the U.S. and then assembles and installs the Fandrich Vertical Action™ from a combination of Chinese, American, and German (Renner) parts. The pianos are also available with a standard Chinese-made action. Fandrich & Sons also sells 5' 9" and 6' 1" grands, modified from Korean-made Hyundai models, and a 7' grand modified from a Guangzhou model. At present, all these pianos are sold primarily in the Seattle area. (Do not confuse these pianos with the original U.S.-made Fandrich piano described under "Fandrich" in *The Piano Book*.) From time to time, Fandrich & Sons also purchases other brands of new vertical and grand pianos and modifies them or installs Fandrich actions.

Fazioli

Fazioli now offers two actions and two pedal lyres as options on all their grand pianos. Having two actions allows for more voicing options without having to constantly revoice the hammers. This could be useful when several players with different requirements must regularly share the same instrument, or for a single player who prefers a radically different sound for certain pieces of music. The second pedal lyre is an option for those pianos outfitted with Fazioli's unique fourth pedal mechanism (see *The Piano Book* for details). Because some pianists may not need the fourth pedal and may be confused by its presence, the optional second lyre contains only the standard three pedals.

Fazioli is building a new factory which will allow the company to modestly increase production, efficiency, and quality control, and which will have a research area with testing equipment and a concert hall.

Feurich / Wilh. Steinberg

New U.S. distributor:

Feurich-Steinberg Pianos USA
9615 W. 128th Terrace
Shawnee Mission, Kansas 66213

913-851-8219

In recent years, until 1998, Feurich grands have been manufactured for the Feurich family by Schimmel. They were identical in most respects to Schimmel grands of the same size, except that the Feurichs benefited from the use of Kluge keys with artificial-ivory keytops, as well as some cosmetic changes to the cabinet. In 1998, manufacture of Feurich pianos was discontinued by Schimmel.

In 1999, Feurich, in search of a factory, and Wilh. Steinberg Pianos, with a factory but in search of financial support, merged to form the Thuringer Pianoforte Co. Both brands will be produced in this factory, in most cases retaining their respective traditional, distinctive scale designs. Production is scheduled to begin in the summer of 1999. Models and prices were not yet available at press time.

Förster, August

New importer/distributor address:

German American Trading Co., Inc.
5008 W. Linebaugh Ave., Suite 36
Tampa, Florida 33624

813-961-8405

Please note that there is a piano sold under the August Förster name in Canada and several European countries which is made by Petrof and is similar to the Petrof piano. Except for the name, it has no connection to the August Förster pianos made in Germany. I'm told that this situation came about because of a legal conflict many years ago over the rights to the August Förster name, which resulted in an agreement specifying in which countries each manufacturer could market pianos under this name.

Fritz Dobbert—See "Dobbert, Fritz"

Gaveau—See "Pleyel / Gaveau"

George Steck—See "Steck, George"

Grinnell Bros.—See "Samick / Kohler & Campbell"

Grotrian

New importer/distributor:

Strings Limited
314 S. Milwaukee Ave., Ste. B
Libertyville, Illinois 60048

847-367-5224
800-580-7768

Several models of vertical piano have been added to the product line.

Hallet, Davis & Co. (new listing)

North American Music, Inc.
126 Route 303
W. Nyack, New York 10994

800-541-2331
914-353-3520

This famous old American piano brand name dates back to at least 1843 and changed hands many times over the years. It eventually became part of the Aeolian group of piano brands, and instruments bearing the name were manufactured at Aeolian's Memphis plant before that company went out of business in 1985. The name is currently being applied to pianos made by Samick in Korea and distributed by Hyundai, and are nearly identical to those sold under Hyundai's Maeari label. See under "Maeari / Hallet & Davis" for models and prices.

Hastings—Name discontinued

Hazelton—See "Samick / Kohler & Campbell"

Hoffmann, W. (new listing)

This piano brand, part of the Bechstein group, was described under "Bechstein, C." in *The Piano Book*. Here is some additional information:

Bechstein makes two lines of piano under the W. Hoffmann name: "Trend" and "World." The Trend series includes all verticals except the 46" model H-117, and are made in a Bechstein-owned factory in Germany. The World series, which includes the H-117 and all the grands, are manufactured in the Czech Republic by Petrof. They use the same scale designs as Petrof pianos, but are built to Bechstein's specifications. After the completion of basic manufacturing, the pianos are sent to Bechstein for additional work, including regulating, voicing, and other final preparation.

Ibach

Soon after the third edition of *The Piano Book* went to press, Daewoo decided not to distribute Korean-made Ibach pianos in the U.S. However, the pianos *are* being distributed in Canada. The Canadian distributor is:

Bingley Distributors
280 Dufferin Ave.
Trenton, Ontario
Canada K8V 5G2

613-394-4729

Jasper (-American)—See "Kimball"

Kawai

Kawai has made extensive changes to its product line in the few years since the third edition of *The Piano Book* was published. As is characteristic of Kawai, the vertical piano line—the console models in particular—can be confusing. Briefly, Kawai's current console line consists only of the 500- and 600-series pianos in furniture-style cabinets. (The 41" model CX-5 and the 44" model CE-11, both in continental style, have been discontinued.) The models 502 and 503 were 42" consoles in simple furniture styles. The latest version, model 505, is 43" in height. The 602, no longer made, was a fancier-looking version of the 502. The model 603 was enlarged to 44" and then redesigned as a distinct scale in model 604. The new 44" model 605 is similar to the 604.

Kawai's least expensive piano at present is the very popular model CX-5H, a 45" piano that Kawai calls a "studio." This model actually has the same scale design as the discontinued 41" model CX-5 console, but the height has been increased to 45" through the use of casters and an extended back. Also like the CX-5, this model has the compressed action typical of a console piano (see page 44 of *The Piano Book* for further explanation). In other words, despite its designation as a "studio," the model CX-5H is essentially a console piano in a studio-size cabinet. Although the extra height may be appealing to some customers, it confers no technical or musical advantage (nor disadvantage). The CX-5H is much less expensively constructed than the CX-5 was, including a laminated mahogany-core soundboard and a less robust back structure. A new variant, model 504, is the same piano in a furniture-style cabinet, but with a shorter, 43" back. These inexpensive models are satisfactory entry-level pianos, but for the reasons mentioned, they may not be quite the bargain they seem initially and are probably not appropriate for more demanding applications, especially if the piano needs to be moved frequently.

Kawai's line of studio pianos remains about the same as described in *The Piano Book*, but the uprights are undergoing some changes. Final specifications were not settled at press time, but it appears that the 48" model CX-21 will be upgraded in cabinetry and action and reissued as model K-30E. The 49" model K-50E will be replacing the NS-20A and the 52" model K-60E will be replacing the US-6X. The K-50E has a thicker back, cabinet style changes, and NEOTEX™ keytops (Kawai's brand of ivory substitute); the K-60E adds agraffes in bass and tenor and a duplex scale. The 52" model US-8X will eventually be discontinued. Prices for the new models were not

17

available at press time, but will reportedly be about the same as the old models.

Kawai has replaced its entire KG and GS series of grands (with the exception of the GS-100) with a new RX series. According to the company, these new pianos have NEOTEX™ keytops, new case beam and plate strut configurations, a scratch-resistant music desk, and new scale designs. The "R" (Artisan Select) series of grands has essentially been phased out, except for the superior model RX-A. (Note that the "R" series mentioned in *The Piano Book* is not the same as the "RX" series; the only point of overlap is the RX-A.) A 7' 6" model RX-7 has been added to the line. Some recent technical changes to the grands include vertically-laminated bridges with bridge caps, a harder inner rim, and more extensive use of ABS Styran in grand action parts.

In other changes, the new model GM-2A (upgraded from the 4' 9" GM-1) is an inexpensive 5' grand with a slightly scaled-down cabinet. A new model GE-1A is the same as the model GE-1, with the addition of a duplex scale. The GE-1AS also has a Soft-Fall fallboard and NEOTEX™ keytops. The 5' 9" model GE-3 grand has replaced the 5' 7" GE-2. To celebrate the company's 70th anniversary, in 1997 Kawai made some of its models, both grand and vertical, available with cosmetic and functional enhancements. These models were marked "Limited Edition" (LE) and are no longer available.

The AnyTime (hybrid digital/acoustic) piano is now available in the models CX-5H (AT-105) vertical and RX-2 (RX-2AT) grand, the other AnyTime models having been discontinued. The AnyTime pianos feature a new sound engine with a new sampling of Kawai's EX concert grand piano. Note that the grand uses optical sensors under the keys, whereas the verticals use button contacts.

Correction: *The Piano Book* is incorrect in stating that the Kawai warranty does not cover broken strings. As with most other brands, string breakage is covered except when due to extremely heavy use or abuse.

Kemble

New U.S. distributor:

Kemble Company LTD
251 Memorial Rd.
Lititz, Pennsylvania 17543

888-3-KEMBLE

Kimball

In February 1996, Kimball announced that it would cease all production of vertical pianos. This completes Kimball's exit from the domestic piano business. In July 1995, Kimball stopped making grands, and for a year or so Kimball verticals were largely built by Baldwin, with only cabinets and final assembly by Kimball. Kimball will continue to honor its warranties, and will also continue to build piano cabinets for other makers, such as Samick and Kawai, as it has for some time now. The company sold most of its piano-making equipment to a Chinese piano manufacturer, with whom, reportedly, it hopes to develop a joint venture in the Chinese market. Kimball International also sold its Herrburger Brooks division in England. However, its Bösendorfer division in Austria is unaffected by these changes.

Kingsburg (new listing)

Piano Wholesalers International, Inc.
4001 SE 45th Court #5
Ocala, Florida 34480

352-694-7761
877-426-5100

Kingsburg pianos are made by the Yantai Longfeng Piano Co. of Yantai City, China. Yantai Longfeng is a relatively small company established in 1991, and is outfitted with automated production equipment from Japan and Germany. Scales for the pianos were developed by German scale designer Klaus Fenner, and some of the piano components come from Japan and Germany.

Knabe, (Wm.) (new listing)

PianoDisc
4111-A North Freeway Blvd.
Sacramento, California 95834

800-566-3472
916-567-9999

The "PianoDisc" line of pianos previously offered by this company has been discontinued and replaced by two new lines of piano resurrecting the Knabe name. Knabe is an old American brand name that eventually became part of the Mason & Hamlin family of brands (see "Mason & Hamlin").

Pianos bearing the name "Wm. Knabe," like the discontinued PianoDisc line, are made by Young Chang in Korea. The piano's cabinet design and appearance have been altered, and the hammers have been changed, resulting in different touch characteristics, the company says. Pianos bearing only the name "Knabe" are made in Young Chang's facility in Tianjin, China. (Wm. Knabe model designations begin with KN; Knabe models begin with KB.) The keybeds for both Knabe and Wm. Knabe pianos are modified at their respective factories for easier installation of a PianoDisc system at a later date, if desired, and the pianos are extensively serviced in PianoDisc's California facility prior to being shipped to dealers.

Knabe and Wm. Knabe pianos can be ordered by the dealer as regular acoustic pianos, or with the PianoDisc or QuietTime systems factory-installed. See under "PianoDisc" in *The Piano Book* and in this *Supplement* for more information on these systems.

Knight, Alfred—See "Whelpdale Maxwell & Codd"

Kohler & Campbell—See "Samick / Kohler & Campbell"

Krakauer

Krakauer Pianos
1175 W. 14th St.
Jasper, Indiana 47546

812-482-4202

The Krakauer name was formerly owned by Kimball. When Kimball ceased piano manufacturing in 1996, it sold the Krakauer name to another party. Today's Krakauer pianos are made by Artfield Piano Ltd., a young Chinese firm that purchased Kimball's piano production equipment. Artfield makes pianos in American furniture-style and European-style cabinets under the Krakauer name. The Krakauer line uses quite a few foreign-made parts, such as Japanese hammers and a German Delignit pinblock. Artfield also makes private-label pianos with all Chinese parts. Some former and present Kimball executives are assisting Artfield in presenting its pianos to the U.S. market.

Maddison (new listing)

This name is no longer in use. The verticals and 5' 2" grand used a strung back and action from the Guangzhou Piano Manufactory in Guangzhou, China. The strung back for the 5' 6" grand came from the Beijing Piano Co. The piano was assembled in Macao using a Macao-made cabinet.

Mason & Hamlin

New phone number: 978-374-8888

In mid-1994, the Mason & Hamlin Companies ceased production of all Mason & Hamlin, Falcone, and Sohmer pianos, and in January 1995 filed for Chapter 7 (liquidation) bankruptcy. Shortly thereafter, a Boston-based piano rebuilding firm, Premier Pianos, obtained the controlling interest in the company from its former owner and persuaded the Bankruptcy Court to change the bankruptcy filing to Chapter 11 (reorganization).

From early 1995 to early 1996, the new owners completed the manufacture of pianos left unfinished when the plant closed, made some new pianos from scratch, and attempted to fight off legal attempts by creditors to force liquidation of the company or its sale to another party. (Many creditors did not have faith in the new owners' ability to put the company back on its feet.) In April 1996, the Court sided with the creditors and approved the sale of Mason & Hamlin to Kirk and Gary Burgett, owners of PianoDisc, makers of electronic player piano systems. The Mason & Hamlin assets also included the Falcone, Sohmer, Knabe, and George Steck brand names and designs.

At the time of this writing, the Burgett brothers are manufacturing Mason & Hamlin pianos once again at the Haverhill, Massachusetts factory, with the design plans used during the company's Boston era (1881-1932). They are making the 50" vertical, as well as the models A and BB grands. In 1999 the company reports that it has begun shipping the A and BB models in satin mahogany as well as ebony, and that all satin finishes are now done in lacquer. These models are also available in a new stylized case design called Monticello, which has fluted, conical legs, similar to a Hepplewhite style, with matching lyre and bench. Monticello is available only in satin mahogany. The warranty on Mason & Hamlin pianos has been extended from ten years to twelve on the soundboard, lifetime on the case and action parts. Initial reports on these instruments are positive.

The Knabe name is being applied to a line of pianos from Korea (see "Knabe"). The George Steck brand name is being used on a line of pianos from Guangzhou, China which are similar to the Pearl River brand (see "Steck, George"). Some of the Mason & Hamlins and many of the Knabes and Stecks are being sold with PianoDisc units installed. Plans for the Falcone and Sohmer brand names are still being discussed.

For those who have a need to know, the serial numbers of the Mason & Hamlin pianos built or completed by the interim (Premier) ownership were from 90590 to 90613 inclusive.

Mecklenburg (new listing)

Mecklenburg Piano Co.
1000 Lake Street, Building D
Ramsey, New Jersey 07446

201-825-7676
888-857-8100

Mecklenburg is the brand name of Klavierfabrik Nordpiano GmbH, established in 1996 in the German state of Mecklenburg with support and subsidies from the German government. At present, the company offers only one piano model—a 48" upright. The piano is sold with two upper panels, one in traditional styling and one in contemporary; the customer can choose which one to use and can change it at any time.

Although final assembly and action installation are performed in Germany, much sub-assembly work and cabinet finishing is done in Russia, enabling the company to sell the piano at an attractive price compared to most other German pianos. The instruments have Delignit pinblocks, Renner actions, and Abel hammers, and the keyboards are from Poland.

Nakamichi / Nakamura

Due to a trademark conflict with the Nakamichi company that sells audio equipment, the Nakamichi piano (no relation) was changed to "Nakamura." Distribution was discontinued in 1998.

Niemeyer (new listing)

North American Music
126 Rt. 303
W. Nyack, New York 10994

914-353-3520
800-541-2331

These pianos are made in China by the Dongbei Piano Co.

Nordiska (new listing)

Geneva International Corp.
29 East Hintz Rd.
Wheeling, Illinois 60090

800-533-2388
847-520-9970

Nordiska was a Swedish piano manufacturer which, upon going out of business, sold all its designs, equipment, and technology to the Chinese company Dongbei. Beginning in 1998, Dongbei's Nordiska-designed piano, as well as other Dongbei models, will be sold in the U.S. under the Nordiska name by Geneva International Corp., the Petrof distributor. The Nordiska-designed model appears to be technically more advanced than the other models Dongbei manufactures. (This model is also sold by Weber under the Sagenhaft label, and possibly by others.)

Pearl River (new listing)

New distributor:

Poppenberg & Associates
966 S. Pearl St.
Denver, Colorado 80209

303-765-5775

These pianos are made by the Guangzhou Piano Manufactory in Guangzhou, China, the largest piano factory in China and one of the largest in the world. This is a return of the Pearl River name, which was present in the U.S. market several years ago, but discontinued because the quality at that time was not good enough to allow the brand to maintain a foothold in the market. With the influx of investment by the Chinese government and foreign businesses, the quality has greatly improved and continues to improve rapidly. Note that the 49" model UP-125 M-1 is a joint venture between Yamaha and Guangzhou. The parts are made by Guangzhou and assembled by Yamaha in a nearby factory. (These pianos are distributed and warranted by Pearl River, not Yamaha.)

Petrof / Weinbach

Petrof now has a 52" upright with a complete Renner action, not available under the Weinbach label. 50" Petrof uprights have Renner action parts on a Petrof action frame.

All 5' 3", 5' 8", and regular 6' 4" Petrof grands contain Renner action parts, assembled onto a Petrof action frame at the Petrof factory. The 7' 9" and 9' 3" models have complete Renner actions. A new 6' 4" model III-M, made in the same factory as the two larger models, also has a complete Renner action, as well as other refinements common to the larger models.

Petrof has switched from Delignit to a 7-ply beech pinblock in its Petrof and Weinbach grands.

Petrof is now introducing the Rösler name into the U.S., a name it uses extensively in Europe. This line of pianos will be less expensive than the Petrof and Weinbach lines. The Rösler models are similar to the Petrof models, but the cabinets have synthetic laminate finishes instead of wood veneer. The middle pedal performs a bass sustain function.

The Petrof factory also makes a piano under the August Förster name, similar to the Petrof but different from the August Förster made in Germany. This Czech August Förster is available in Canada and several European countries, but not in the U.S. See under "Förster, August" for more information.

Geneva International, the Petrof distributor in the U.S., is also importing a line of Chinese pianos under the Nordiska label. See under "Nordiska."

PianoDisc

The PianoDisc line of pianos has been discontinued and replaced with the Knabe line. See "Knabe."

Concerning the PianoDisc player piano systems, the new model "PDS-128 Plus" plays both floppy disks and their specialized PianoCD software. The unit has a floppy disk drive, and by attaching a CD player you can play the PianoCDs from the same control unit. One channel of the PianoCD contains the digital information that operates the piano playback, while the other channel contains actual audio vocals and accompaniment that play through your speakers. Options still include TFT MIDI Record, the SymphonyPro Sound Module (now with 16 megabytes of memory and 64-note polyphony), and amplified speakers, as well as the PianoMute Rail from the new QuietTime system (see below) to "turn off" the acoustic piano sound if desired. The less-expensive "PianoCD" system is available, without a floppy disk drive, for those customers who desire to play only PianoCDs. All systems feature a full dynamic range of 127 levels of expression. A new optional radio-frequency remote control with backlit keypad and LCD display, called "ProControl," will be available in Fall, 1999.

The latest version of the PDS-128 Plus incorporates new "SilentDrive" technology, circuitry that allows much closer control of the key and pedal solenoids. The new units are said to operate more quietly, and to provide better volume control and faster key and pedal response than before. The system is now compatible with virtually all Standard MIDI file software.

In 1999, PianoDisc added Music Expansion (MX) to the PDS-128 Plus. MX utilizes flash technology, a non-volatile form of memory, to store hours of music—over a thousand songs—and play them back without ever having to change a disk. Music can be recorded to MX from many formats, including PianoDisc software, MIDI files, or from the piano keyboard. Songs can then be separated into as many as twelve individual libraries. (PianoDisc operating software is upgradeable through the same MX technology.)

"PianoDigital with QuietTime" is PianoDisc's newest system. QuietTime turns a piano into a hybrid acoustic/digital instrument. In regular mode, the piano plays just like an ordinary piano. If desired, the system will provide orchestrated accompaniment through amplified speakers. When the QuietTime feature is activated, the acoustic sound is turned off (the PianoMute rail prevents the hammers from hitting the strings) and the digital piano and other instrumental sounds are turned on and can be accessed using stereo headphones (perfect for late-night playing). Two headphone jacks are supplied. Like the PianoDisc system, QuietTime can be installed into just about any piano.

The QuietTime model GT-360 supplies 128 different General MIDI instrumental sounds, 16 megabytes of memory, 64-note polyphony, MIDI In, Out & Thru, 16 MIDI channels with reverb and other effects, key range settings, and the ability to create and save up to 75 of your own custom sound-combination presets. The less expensive model GT-90 has 16 instrumental selections which are factory pre-set, and the ability to make 40 possible sound combinations. The emphasis on this model is simplicity of operation, as most functions can be accessed by pushing one or two buttons. QuietTime has been redesigned so that it can be fully integrated with the PianoDisc system.

For price information, see the Model and Pricing Guide section of this *Supplement* under "PianoDisc."

Pleyel / Gaveau (new listing)

Sandell Trading Co.
600 Mandalay Avenue
Clearwater Beach, Florida 33767

877-771-7001 (toll-free)
727-442-1933

Pleyel and Company manufactures Pleyel, Rameau, and Gaveau pianos in Provence in the south of France. Although pianos have been made under these names since 1807, Pleyel and Gaveau were made by Schimmel (and were pretty much identical to Schimmel pianos) from 1971 to 1994. In that year the contract with Schimmel was terminated and the pianos were once again returned to France, where they are now made to different designs. The Rameau brand is not currently being imported into the U.S.

All Pleyel models, and the largest two Gaveau models, have Renner actions; the other Gaveau models contain Langer actions. The Pleyel grands use Renner hammers. All Pleyel and Gaveau pianos use Delignit pinblocks.

QRS / Pianomation

The Pianomation system can now be configured in a variety of ways. As before, the customer can use his or her own regular CD player, which can be controlled with an optional wireless remote. QRS also now makes a more sophisticated CD-ROM drive that fits under the keybed of the piano. If desired, the unit can be purchased with a 3.5" floppy disk drive instead of, or in addition to, the CD-ROM drive. (The units that fit under the keybed cannot at present be controlled with the wireless remote.) The floppy disk drive can read Standard MIDI files and so is compatible with virtually all music software on the market, including software made for the Yamaha Disklavier and for PianoDisc.

As before, Pianomation is available with Orchestration and Record options. When a Pianomation CD is played with the Orchestration option, one channel of the CD contains the digital information that operates the piano playback, while the other channel contains actual audio vocals and accompaniment that play through your speakers. The Pianomation CD library includes live recordings of major symphony orchestras as accompaniment for the piano. The processor has been upgraded to generate a greater range of expression from the number of expression levels available from the CDs. A new optically-sensing version of the Record option is now available. It bounces light off the bottom of the keys to determine their velocity.

QRS offers a version of Pianomation called "Playola," which sits atop the keys (like the "Vorsetzer" of the player piano's halcyon days) and plays the keys with little rubber fingers, either alone or accompanied by orchestral music. Unlike Pianomation, Playola does not operate the pedals. Instead, quasi-pedal ("Magic Pedal") information is incorporated into the software and simulates the pedals through the control of note duration. This simulation is not as realistic as actually controlling the damper pedal, but should probably be sufficient for simpler applications. Playola comes with a carrying case and does not require professional installation by a technician.

QRS' new "Lite Switch" system turns a regular piano into a hybrid digital/acoustic one. When activated, a mute rail stops the hammers from hitting the strings and a sound module containing twelve digital instrumental sounds is turned on. A MIDI strip mounts under the keys.

For price information on Pianomation, Playola, and Lite Switch systems, see the Model and Pricing Guide section of this *Supplement* under "QRS / Pianomation."

A new product called "Presto-Digitation" turns an old upright into a digital piano. A technician removes the old keys and action and replaces them with a kit consisting of a new keyboard, electronics, speakers, and a user interface. This may be a suitable fate for an older piano that would otherwise be discarded. The suggested retail price, including installation, is about $2,300. Installation takes about three hours.

Ridgewood (new listing)

Weber Piano Co.
40 Seaview Drive
Secaucus, New Jersey 07094

800-346-5351
201-902-0920

This name is being applied to verticals, and to 5' 2" and 7' grands, made by the Guangzhou Piano Manufactory in Guangzhou, China.

Rieger-Kloss—See "Bohemia / Rieger-Kloss"

Rösler—See "Petrof / Weinbach"

Sagenhaft (new listing)

Weber Piano Co.
40 Seaview Drive
Secaucus, New Jersey 07094

800-346-5351
201-902-0920

This piano name was listed under "Weber" in *The Piano Book*, but is now being given its own listing. The verticals are all made by the Chinese piano manufacturer Dongbei. The S-116 models are Nordiska designs, purchased from the Swedish company of the same name (as mentioned in the book); the other models are Dongbei's own designs. The Nordiska models are clearly the better of the two. The model S-112 is a "deluxe" version of Dongbei's S-111 designed especially for Sagenhaft. It contains tone escapements, and end panels redesigned for greater physical stability.

The Sagenhaft 5' 5" grand is also made by Dongbei, using equipment purchased from the Korean company that used to make Sojin pianos.

Samick / Kohler & Campbell

A few years ago, Samick added Kluge keys, Renner actions, and Renner or Abel hammers to its four largest grand piano models (6' 1", 6' 8", 7' 4", 9' 1") and designated them as its "World Piano" series (models began with the letters WSG). According to the company, these models also received extra pre-sale preparation in the U.S. before being shipped to dealers. In Samick's Kohler & Campbell line, the 6' 10" and 7' models were "World Pianos" (no special model designation), though only the 7' had the full complement of features. The 6' 10" grand used Samick keys, Renner action, and Renner hammers.

In 1999, Samick revised its World Piano series. In the Samick line, World verticals (WSV) have spruce back posts, a slow-close fallboard, and agraffes (and a sostenuto pedal in the 52" size). World grands (now using the letters WFG), in addition to Kluge keys, Renner action, and Abel or Imadegawa hammers, also have a whole assortment of features similar to those in some high-end pianos, such as a seven-ply rock maple pinblock fitted to the plate flange, no tuning pin bushings, vertically laminated maple bridges with maple cap, solid maple legs with leg plates, and a triangle shoe "tone collector," among others. As with all Samick pianos, the soundboard is a veneer-type laminated board.

In the Kohler & Campbell line, the revised World Piano series has been renamed "Millennium." Millennium verticals (MKV) have the same features as World verticals except that the soundboard is tapered solid spruce. Millennium grands (KFM) have the same features as the revised World grands, except that in the Millenniums the strings are all individually hitched, the soundboard is tapered solid spruce, and there is no duplex scale.

Other changes to the Samick grand piano line include: adding a 4' 11-1/2" grand model SG-150, discontinuing the 5' 1" model, and replacing it with a 5' 3-1/2" model SG-161. The 5' 1" model remains, however, in the Kohler & Campbell line. Hardwood legs with iron leg plates (for greater physical stability), a slow-close fallboard, a spruce-veneered keybed (for greater resistance to warpage), and rims made of alternating layers of maple and luan (for greater hardness) are additions to both the Samick and Kohler & Campbell regular series of grands.

Samick has opened a factory in Indonesia for the production of guitars and pianos. The pianos currently being offered from Indonesia are those with model numbers beginning with JS (verticals) and SIG (grands) in the Samick line and KC (verticals) and KIG (grands) in the Kohler & Campbell line. These Indonesian-assembled pianos combine keys, actions, hammers, and plates from Korea with soundboards and cabinets from Indonesia. The laminated soundboards on the smaller verticals are made of agatis, a wood indigenous to Indonesia also used for guitar soundboards (veneered spruce is used on the larger verticals and the grands). Pianos destined for U.S. dealers are first prepared for sale by Samick in California before being shipped to their final destination. During 1996–97, the name "Hazelton" was briefly used on a 43" console assembled in Korea using materials from the Indonesian factory.   Once the new factory came fully online, the Hazelton model was discontinued.

Samick makes several private-label brands for individual dealers. A name not previously reported on in these pages is "Grinnell Bros.," a company that manufactured pianos in the midwest from 1902 to about 1960. The name is now owned and used by a Detroit-area piano dealer, Hammell Music. Pianos bearing that name are made by Samick and are similar in features to pianos in the Kohler & Campbell line.

In 1996, Samick filed for bankruptcy protection with the Korean courts under a code similar to Chapter 11 in the U.S. Although its music operations have been profitable and its products have been in demand, several unprofitable non-music subsidiaries left Samick strapped for cash and saddled with debt. The Korean courts have approved Samick's reorganization plan, allowing the company to sell off its non-music subsidiaries and continue in business. The manufacture of Samick pianos and their distribution in the U.S. have not been materially affected by the bankruptcy action.

Sängler & Söhne / Wieler

New importer/distributor address:

North American Music
126 Rt. 303
W. Nyack, New York 10994

914-353-3520
800-541-2331

At present, the 43", 44", and 45" pianos bearing these names are made by the Guangzhou Piano Manufactory in Guangzhou, China. The 47" pianos are made in Belarus. These pianos are also available to dealers with a name of their choice; some sample names are Ackermann, Langston, Steiff & Sohne, and Rohrbach.

Sauter

Sauter has introduced versions of its 48" upright and 6' 1" grand with cabinets designed by the famous European designer Peter Maly.

The 7' 3" model 220 grand has some unusual features that at first glance seem to be only decorative, but turn out to be functional. Colored lines painted on the soundboard and white inlays on the tops of the dampers act as guides to musicians performing music for "prepared piano"—that is, ultra-modern music requiring the insertion of foreign objects between the strings or the plucking or striking of strings directly by the performer. The colored lines indicate to the performer where to touch the strings to produce certain harmonics. The white inlays on certain dampers indicate the location of the black keys for easier navigation around the "keyboard" when accessing the strings directly. This model reportedly had its origin as a custom-made instrument for the Paris Conservatory. When it met with approval, it was integrated into the Sauter line.

Schimmel

Schimmel has discontinued selling its 5' 1" grand.

In 1997, the company introduced a new 6' grand model 182 to replace the 5' 10" model 174. Various tonal enhancemnents were made to the plate, soundboard, and scale design, and the new model uses the keys and action from Schimmel's 6' 10" grand. The slightly longer case of the new model was necessary to accommodate the longer keys of this action, which, Schimmel says, will give the new piano a more professional "feel" at the keyboard. The 5' 10" model has been discontinued.

All Schimmel grands now have duplex scaling.

In 1999, Schimmel introduced its "Diamond" series of grands and uprights. The Diamond grands, in both the 6' and 6' 10" sizes, are technically the same as the regular series, but have fancier cabinet and plate features and detailing, and are available in a variety of exotic woods. The 49" Diamond upright is a completely new design, both technically and aesthetically. For greater sound volume and longer decay, the soundboard shape, bridge positions, and pinblock arrangement have been designed more like those in a grand piano, according to Schimmel. In the Diamond Noblesse model, the decorative center panel in the bottom door can be exchanged, with a variety of exotic woods to choose from. In the Diamond Prestige model, all the panels in both the bottom and top doors can be exchanged, with striking results.

Schirmer & Son

New phone number: 800-942-5801

In 1997, Schirmer & Son added three grands—5' 4", 6' 3", and 9'—to its previously all-vertical piano line. They are made by Estonia and are similar to the Estonia-brand grands, except that the two smaller Schirmer & Sons grands use Czech actions (the 9' grand uses a Renner action). In addition, there are some cosmetic changes requested by Schirmer. New models of grands from the same factory that makes the verticals (in Poland), including models with wood finishes, will be available in late 1999. Models and prices were not available at press time.

Note that the Th. Betting piano line, which was identical to the Schirmer & Son line, has been discontinued.

Schubert (new listing)

Tri-Con Music Group
1626 North Prospect Ave. #2006
Milwaukee, Wisconsin 53202

941-953-9628
800-336-9164

This name was used for a brief period several years ago on an off-brand Korean piano. Currently, the name is used on pianos from Belarus. Features include an all-spruce back, Delignit pinblock, and solid spruce soundboard.

Schultz & Sons

As mentioned in *The Piano Book*, Schultz & Sons pianos are joint ventures, with established piano manufacturers, in which Schultz adds technical improvements of its own to the manufacturers' regular models. The most recent additions to the Schultz & Sons line (projected for fall 1999) are manufactured by Samick in Korea and by Whelpdale Maxwell & Codd under the Broadwood label in England. Schultz says the Samick pianos are ordered with an assortment of specifications from the upscale "World" and "Millennium" series in the Samick and Kohler & Campbell lines, i.e., with Renner actions, Renner or Abel hammers, Kluge keys, and higher quality soundboard material, as well as with some additional modifications unique to the Schultz & Sons line that vary from model to model. Then, Schultz says, for both the Samick and Broadwood pianos, in its own facility it makes scaling and damper refinements to improve tone, adds steel reinforcement to the vertical backpost and grand beam structures to enhance tuning stability, and calibrates the touch weight to make the action more responsive. Schultz reports that its line of pianos will be sold at selected department stores along the east coast of the U.S. in addition to regular piano outlets.

Schulze Pollmann (new listing)

North American Music Inc.
126 Route 303
W. Nyack, New York 10994

800-541-2331
914-353-3520

Schulze Pollmann was formed in 1928 by the merger of two German piano builders who had moved to Italy, where the company still resides today. Since 1973 the firm has been owned by Generalmusic, which is best known for its digital pianos and organs and other musical electronics. Schulze Pollmann utilizes both sophisticated technology and hand work in its manufacturing. The pianos contain Delignit pinblocks and Renner actions, among other features.

Seiler

The importer/distributor, formerly called Seiler America, has changed its name, address, and phone number to:

Prestige Pianos International, Inc.
7550 Slate Ridge Blvd.
Columbus, Ohio 43068

614-866-2605

Seiler's 48" and 52" uprights are now available with the optional "Super Magnet Repetition" (SMR) action, a patented feature that uses magnets to increase repetition speed. Tiny magnets are attached to certain action parts of each note. During playing, the magnets repel each other, forcing the parts to return to their rest position faster, ready for a new key stroke.

Optional on all Seiler pianos is the patented "Duo Vox" system that can turn a regular piano into a hybrid acoustic/digital instrument (similar to the Yamaha MIDIPiano or "Silent Series" pianos). A key sensor system interfaces with a sound module to provide the digitized sound of a concert grand at the touch of a button. A lever-actuated "acoustic mute" rail completely silences the piano by preventing the hammers from hitting the strings, or the regular muffler rail can be used for quiet acoustic-piano playing, if desired. Headphone jacks for private listening and MIDI ports for interfacing with peripherals are also provided.

Seiler now uses its Membrator system (specially tapered soundboard) and Tonal Volume Stabilizer (equalized tension across bridges) on its verticals as well as grands. A slow-close fallboard is used on all grands. A new "Elite Trainer" model is a digital piano with a real (acoustic) piano action, including real piano hammers, for a realistic feel.

Sohmer—See "Mason & Hamlin"

Steck, George (new listing)

PianoDisc
4111-A North Freeway Blvd.
Sacramento, California 95834

800-566-3472
916-567-9999

George Steck was an old American brand name that eventually became part of the Mason & Hamlin family of brands, along with Knabe and others (see "Mason & Hamlin"). The name is now being applied to a line of Chinese pianos from the Guangzhou factory. The pianos are said to be similar to those sold under the Pearl River name. They are made factory-ready for installation of a PianoDisc system, if desired, and are serviced at the PianoDisc factory in Sacramento, California prior to being shipped to dealers.

Steigerman (new listing)

Steigerman Music Corp.
300A - 750 Terminal Ave.
Vancouver, British Columbia
Canada V6A 2M5

604-921-6217

The Steigerman name is owned by Robert Loewen, a Canadian distributor. Over the last several decades, Loewen has used the Steigerman name on pianos from several manufacturers, including Yamaha and, more recently, Samick, imported into Canada. He also imports pianos from a variety of Chinese companies onto which dealers can place their own house-brand names.

For the past several years, Steigerman pianos have been made by the Yantai Longfeng Piano Co. of Yantai City, China. Steigerman discontinued importing the Yantai Longfeng pianos in 1998. The next generation of Steigerman pianos will be made in Young Chang's Tianjin, China factory and in the Beijing Piano Company factory, according to the importer, and will be distributed primarily in Canada. Models and prices were not available at press time.

Steinberg, Wilh.—See "Feurich / Wilh. Steinberg"

Steingraeber & Söhne

New U.S. contact:

Chris Finger Pianos
101 Second Ave.
P.O. Box 623
Niwot, Colorado 80544

303-652-3110

This small German piano maker (about 250 pianos per year) is once again actively marketing in the U.S. after an absence of a few years. In addition to the review in *The Piano Book*, here is some additional information that may be useful:

Steingraeber makes four sizes of vertical piano. The largest is 54" tall, one of the largest uprights made today. The 51" upright features a special action with a patented repetition mechanism. The company also makes two sizes of grand piano, 5' 6" and 6' 9". The 5' 6" model has an unusually wide tail, allowing for a larger soundboard and longer bass strings than is customary for an instrument of its size.

Steingraeber is willing to make custom cabinets and finishes. They also specialize in so-called ecological or biological finishes, available as an option on most models. This involves the use of only organic materials in the piano, such as natural paints and glues in the case, and white keytops made from cattle bone.

Steinway & Sons

In April 1995, Steinway Musical Properties, Inc., parent corporation of Steinway & Sons, was purchased by Selmer Industries, Inc., parent corporation of The Selmer Company, a major manufacturer of band instruments. The new combined company, known as Steinway Musical Instruments, Inc., is now listed on the New York Stock Exchange. Management at Steinway & Sons remains the same.

It is well known that Steinway's principal competition comes from used and rebuilt Steinways. The company has responded by reissuing old, turn-of-the-century designs, available in models L (5' 10-1/2") and B (6' 10-1/2"), a series of pianos Steinway calls "Limited Editions." The Limited Edition model issued in 1995, known as "Instrument of the Immortals," was actually an amalgam of several different Victorian-era designs, including round, "ice-cream cone" legs; an elaborately carved music desk; and raised beads on the case and around the plate holes; among other features. All examples of this model have been sold.

The 1997 release, informally known as "Sketch 390," commemorates the 200th anniversary of the birth of Steinway founder Heinrich Engelhard Steinway. Based on a 1903 design by J.B. Tiffany, only two instruments in this design were originally manufactured, one of which survives today. It was discovered when it came into the Steinway Restoration Department for rebuilding. This design features over forty feet of hand-carved moldings on the lid, case edges, and legs in "Tulip" and "Egg & Dart" patterns. Production of this model is limited to two hundred instruments in East Indian Rosewood and African Pommele, models L and B only.

In 1998, Steinway continued its long tradition of building custom art case pianos with the commissioning of noted furniture designer Frank Pollaro to create an art case in French art deco style for a model B grand. In 1999, Pollaro designed an art case piano called "Rhapsody" to commemorate the 100th anniversary of the birth of George Gershwin. The piano features a blue-dyed maple veneer adorned with more than 400 hand-cut mother-of-pearl stars, and a gilded silver plate. Several other art case pianos were also built in 1999. The art case instruments are said to be the crowning piece in Steinway's pyramid of models, the other levels being (from bottom to top) Boston pianos, regular model Steinway pianos, Steinway Crown Jewel Collection pianos with exotic veneers (now also available on verticals), and Limited Edition Steinway pianos, mentioned above, that are reproductions of older designs. Steinway says it would like to cultivate collaborations between itself, its clients, and furniture designers in the creation of custom art case instruments.

Effective immediately, a "satin lustre" finish is standard on all Steinway grands in natural wood finishes (i.e., not ebony). Satin lustre is Steinway's name for a finish that is in between satin and high-polish in glossiness. Satin continues to be the standard finish for ebony pianos.

Steinway has released a computer CD called "An Interactive Factory Tour" containing more than one hundred photos and video clips illustrating how its instruments are made. To obtain a copy, call or visit your local Steinway dealer. Technicians can buy it from the Steinway Parts Department.

In 1999, Steinway acquired the Herman Kluge company, Europe's largest manufacturer of piano keys, which supplies keys for Steinway pianos. The number of suppliers of piano keys and actions has been dwindling; this acquisition ensures the availability of this vital component for Steinway.

Story & Clark

Story & Clark now makes a 5' 5" grand (the "Hampton") in the U.S. This piano is unusual in that unlike most grand rims, which are made as one continuous piece bent around a form, its maple rim is made in four pieces, glued and doweled together. The piano has German Abel hammers with a Czech- and Renner-made action, and comes in several different furniture styles.

Story & Clark imports several models from China. The 44" console, 46" studio, and 5' 6" grand, all called "Prelude," are made by the Dongbei Piano Co. All the larger vertical models (up to 55") and the 4' 8" and 5' 6" grands, called "Cambridge," are made by the Beijing Piano Co. There are also 4' 7" and 5' 1" grands (models 47 and 51) made in Korea by Samick, similar to those sold under the Hyundai label.

Story & Clark is part of the QRS company. See under "QRS" for more information on this company's products.

Strauss (new listing)

L & M International, Inc.
6452 Bresslyn Rd.
Nashville, Tennessee 37205

615-356-3686

Strauss pianos are made by the Shanghai Piano Co. in Shanghai, China. The oldest piano manufacturer in China, Shanghai is said to have been founded over a hundred years ago by the British. The name was changed to Shanghai when the Communists took over China around 1950.

Shanghai makes pianos under a number of different names. The name currently used on pianos for export to the U.S. is "Strauss." In the recent past, the name "Nieer" was sometimes used. Pianos can also be special-ordered with the name "Helios."

Walter, Charles R.

The "Janssen" line of consoles has been discontinued. The Walter 6' 4" grand is now available.

Weber

Weber has added several models made in Young Chang's new factory in Tianjin, China (see "Young Chang"). In the model listing, these are the models with three-digit numbers (denoting centimeters). Models with two-digit numbers are still made in Young Chang's factory in Korea.

Weber also markets different lines of pianos under the names Sagenhaft, Ridgewood, Bohemia, and Rieger-Kloss (see under those entries).

Weinbach—See "Petrof/Weinbach"

Welmar—See "Whelpdale Maxwell & Codd"

Whelpdale Maxwell & Codd (new listing)

Whelpdale Maxwell & Codd Ltd.
154 Clapham Park Road
London SW4 7DE England

(44) 171 978 2444

This firm is the manufacturer and distributor of Knight, Broadwood, Bentley, and Welmar pianos. After an absence of a few years, they are once again actively distributing in the U.S. The Alfred Knight models are said to be substantially the same as those described in *The Piano Book*. Originally established in 1728, John Broadwood & Sons is one of the oldest and best-known piano brand names, having played an important part in the early history of the piano. The current Broadwoods are of modern design, of course, including four vertical models and one grand. The Welmar and Bentley names are less well known than the other brands in the U.S., but are built to similar standards and are available to dealers who wish to carry additional piano lines. For price information, see each brand under its own name in the Pricing Guide section.

Wieler—See "Sängler & Söhne / Wieler"

Woodchester (new listing)

Unique Pianos, Inc.
223 E. New Haven Ave.
Melbourne, Florida 32901

800-771-6770
407-725-6770

This English company was founded in 1994 on the site of the old Bentley piano factory, which was abandoned when Bentley was purchased by another company. Some of the old Bentley workforce continues to work for Woodchester.

Woodchester manufactures vertical pianos from 44" to 48" in height. The larger models have Renner actions, Abel hammers, Delignit pinblocks, and backs based on a Rippen design. Components for the smaller models are from Poland and the Czech Republic.

Wurlitzer—See "Baldwin"

Yamaha

In Yamaha's regular piano line, the models G1 and G2 grands (5' 3" and 5' 8") have been replaced by models C1 and C2 of the same size. The change is mostly in name; technically the new models are very similar to the old. In addition to the established 5' 3" model GH1B, customers can now choose from a new 5' 3" model GP1 grand, which is the same as the model GH1B, but with a less expensive cabinet. The 4' 11" model A1 has been replaced by the model GA1 of the same size, in a cabinet like that of the GP1. In preparation for the start of grand piano manufacturing in Yamaha's Thomaston, Georgia plant, the 5' 3" model GH1FP (the GH1B in French Provincial style) is being imported from Japan manufactured but unassembled, and then finished and assembled in Thomaston.

Polyester finishes are now being applied in Thomaston. This will allow the company to manufacture and finish cabinet styles there that previously could only be made in Japan. The first model to receive this treatment is the new 45" vertical T116, which is the same instrument as the 45" P2F piano, but in a furniture style more like that of the model U1. The cabinet for the ebony version is made and finished in Taiwan, then shipped to the U.S. for final assembly, but the mahogany version is entirely made and finished in Thomaston.

In other vertical piano changes, a new 44" model M450 supplements the model M500 of the same size and design, but with a less expensive cabinet. A new 48" model T121 supplements the model U1, and is similar to the U1 inside, but with a less expensive cabinet made in Taiwan and sent to Japan for final assembly. The 48" model WX1 and the 52" model WX7 have been discontinued, but the 48" model U1 has been redesigned to contain the scale design and some of the features of the WX1. A new 52" model U5 has been created to embody the scaling and some of the features of the WX7, including agraffes, duplex scaling, and sostenuto. Neither model, however, has the X-shaped back of the WX series. Minor changes have been made to the 52" model U3. All three upright models now have Yamaha's "Slo-Close" fallboard.

Yamaha has renamed its "Silent Series" pianos "MIDIPianos" to emphasize the MIDI feature for marketing purposes. Many Yamaha models are now available as MIDIPianos; model numbers begin with "MP."

In 1997, the Mark II Disklavier system became the Mark IIXG. The "XG" stands for "extended General MIDI" and refers to the new internal tone card that contains an enormous library of 676 voices and numerous special effects from which thousands of combinations can be created by users and programmers. Other new features of the Mark IIXG: MIDI files can be downloaded from any source and up to 1.44 megabytes (about three hours of music) can be stored on a built-in memory chip (upgradeable to 16 megs); the disk drive now reads both high-density and double-density floppy disks; the control unit's ROM is software-upgradeable; and the unit can read Standard MIDI files and so is compatible with all player piano software on the market that adheres to that standard. Note that a few of Yamaha's less expensive grand Disklavier models are available as playback units only, with no recording capabilities. Their model numbers contain the "XG," but not the "II."

New in 1998 was the "Pro" line of Disklaviers, intended for use by recording studios and others with sophisticated recording requirements. The playback solenoid system on the Pro line contains a servo mechanism that continuously monitors performance. Most importantly, the unit can record and playback the release of notes as well as their attack, resulting in a musical rendition much more faithful to the original. The Disklavier Pro line is available on selected grand models over six feet and will contain all the features of the present Disklavier product, as well as the "silent" feature of the MIDIPianos.

A note is in order concerning Yamaha's model numbering system, which is becoming unwieldy due to the proliferation of digital/acoustic products. As new Disklavier models are created, the "IIXG" designation will be dropped to simplify numbering. Thus, the 48" vertical Disklavier model MX100 IIXG has become simply model MX1, and the same piano with the "silent" feature is model MPX1. This simplification has not yet come to the regular grand piano Disklavier line, which continues to use the "IIXG" designation, but grand Disklaviers with the "silent" feature are models DC1S, DC2S, and DC3S, and then DC3PRO, DC5PRO, etc. in the Disklavier Pro line. (A subtle point: Disklaviers with the "silent" feature are *not* called MIDIPianos because *all* Disklaviers have MIDI capabilities. Rather, they are called "Disklaviers with Silent Feature.")

A clarification: Yamaha's Service Bond program encourages Yamaha dealers to provide customers with follow-up service during the first six months of ownership by reimbursing the dealers for part of the cost of providing that service. Yamaha strongly urges its dealers to participate in this program. The program is voluntary, however, and it's possible that a dealer that sells a piano at a large discount might choose to save money by not promising or providing service under the Service Bond program. When negotiating the sale, a customer should inquire as to whether the dealer participates in the Service Bond program. If so, the customer should make sure the service is actually provided. Service for which the dealer can be reimbursed does not include a full action regulation as implied in *The Piano Book*, but does include two tunings and a general maintenance check.

Yamaha operates a joint-venture factory in Guangzhou, China in which it assembles pianos using parts from the nearby Guangzhou Piano Manufactory (maker of Pearl River pianos), as well as parts of its own from Japan and

China. These pianos are sold in other parts of the world under the Yamaha name, but in the U.S. they appear only under the name "Eterna." Currently, this name is applied by Yamaha only to a 44" console patterned after its model M1F. This model is backed by a Yamaha warranty. (Note: Yamaha also assembles a 49" vertical in this factory, made entirely from Guangzhou parts. This model is distributed and warranted by Pearl River under its own name and is not part of the Yamaha line. See under "Pearl River.") Yamaha has also just opened its own solely-funded factory in China, but this factory makes only action parts.

Young Chang

New address and phone:

Young Chang America, Inc.
P.O. Box 99995
Lakewood, Washington 98499

253-589-3200
800-874-2880

In 1995, Young Chang built a new $40 million piano factory in Tianjin, China. Unlike most other Chinese joint ventures, Young Chang chose to design and build the factory from scratch rather than try to reform an existing manufacturing facility. The new Tianjin factory makes two different lines of piano for export to the U.S. The regular line is known as the "Heritage" series. A less-expensive version is sold under the "Bergmann" label (new in 1999). Both versions are assembled from a Chinese back, plate, and cabinet, and a Korean-made action, but the Heritage series uses a solid Chinese spruce soundboard and has Young Chang's fifteen-year full warranty, whereas the Bergmann contains a veneer-type laminated soundboard, uses some plastic (ABS) parts in the action, and has a ten-year limited warranty. Chinese-made vertical model numbers begin with the letters "E," "AF," and "LC;" grands begin with "TG." For Bergmann prices, see under "Bergmann" in the Pricing Guide section.

Young Chang has issued new versions of several of its Korean-made models. The new models have been reengineered by Joseph Pramberger, a former Steinway engineer and manufacturing executive. In most cases, they utilize the same scale designs as the older models, but the bridges, soundboard, and hammers have been redesigned, the actions have been refined in some cases, and there are a number of cosmetic changes to the cabinet and plate. Examples of these models that I've played have sounded better than the older ones. Model numbers for all the improved models begin with the letter "P." Note that, at present, the pianos Young Chang makes for other manufacturers and distributors are the regular (non-Pramberger) models, known as the "Gold" series.

OTHER TOPICS

Humidity Control

Dampp-Chaser Electronics Corp., which manufactures humidity-control equipment for pianos, has introduced several new models and enhancements, including systems that provide humidity control at the back of a vertical piano (where the design of the piano prevents placement of the system inside the front); systems that control humidity at both the back and front, for maximum protection; systems especially designed for climates that are unusually wet or unusually dry; and a "smart" heating element in the humidifier that turns itself off when no water is detected on the cloth pads.

Reduced-Size Keyboard For Small Hands

Pianists with small hands now have a solution to their problem. A 7/8-size keyboard—one in which the width of each key, and therefore the width of the entire keyboard, is 7/8 that of a standard keyboard—is being offered by American manufacturer David Steinbuhler. Although no piano manufacturer yet has this as a factory-supplied option in new pianos, the keyboard can be retrofitted into existing pianos. Steinbuhler is also exploring the possibility of manufacturing other sizes of keyboard and says he can custom-make keyboards to fit any hand.

To have a grand piano retrofitted with the new keyboard, the old keyframe, keyboard, and action are shipped to Steinbuhler's shop, where the old keyframe's size is precisely duplicated, and the new keyframe is fitted with the new keyboard. The action, new keyframe, and new keyboard are returned to the customer, where a local technician slides them back into the piano and regulates everything. The cost of having a 7/8-size keyboard retrofitted into a grand piano is approximately five thousand dollars, and so is most appropriate for serious pianists with high-quality instruments. For more information, contact: Steinbuhler and Co., 600 North Brown St., Titusville, PA 16354; phone (814) 827-0296.

Pianos, Bed & Breakfast

The "Pianos, Bed & Breakfast" program described in *The Piano Book* has been discontinued.

MODEL and PRICING GUIDE

This guide contains the "list price" for nearly every brand, model, style, and finish of new piano that has regular distribution in the United States and, for the most part, Canada. Some marginal, local, or "stencil" brands are omitted. Except where indicated, prices are in U.S. dollars and the pianos are assumed to be for sale in the U.S. (Canadians will find the information useful after translation into Canadian dollars, but there may be differences in import duties and sales practices that will affect retail prices.) Prices and specifications are, of course, subject to change. Most manufacturers revise their prices at least once a year; two or three times a year is not uncommon when currency exchange rates are unstable. The prices in this edition were compiled in the spring of 1999.

Some terms used in this guide require special explanation and disclaimers:

List Price

The list price is usually a starting point for negotiation, not a final sales price. The term "list price," as used in this *Supplement*, is a "standard" list price computed from the published wholesale price according to a formula commonly used in the industry. Some manufacturers use a different formula, however, for their own suggested retail prices, usually one that raises the prices above "standard" list by ten to fifteen percent so that their dealers can advertise a larger "discount" without losing profit. For this reason, price-shopping by comparing discounts from the manufacturers' own suggested retail prices may result in a faulty price comparison. To provide a level playing field for comparing prices, most prices in this guide are computed according to a uniform "standard" formula, *even though it may differ from the manufacturers' own suggested retail prices.* [Exception: Most Steinway suggested retail prices are *lower* than "standard" list, but I'm using Steinway's own prices in this guide because in many cases they are close to the actual selling prices, and comparison shopping is not as big an issue as it is with other brands.] Where my list prices and those of a manufacturer differ, then, no dishonesty should be inferred; we simply employ different formulas. For most models, the price includes a bench and the standard manufacturer's warranty for that brand (see *The Piano Book* for details). Most dealers will also include moving and one or two tunings in the home, but these are optional and a matter of agreement between you and the dealer.

Style and Finish

Unless otherwise indicated, the cabinet style is assumed to be "traditional" and is not stated. Exactly what "traditional" means varies from brand to brand. In general, it is a "classic" styling with minimal embellishment and straight legs. The vertical pianos have front legs, which are free-standing on smaller verticals and attached to the cabinet with toe blocks on larger verticals. "Continental" or European styling refers to vertical pianos without decorative trim and usually without front legs. Other furniture styles (Chippendale, French Provincial, Queen Anne, etc.) are as noted. The manufacturer's own trademarked style name is used when an appropriate generic name could not be determined.

Unless otherwise stated, all finishes are assumed to be "satin," which reflects light but not images. "Polished" finishes, also known as "high-gloss" or "high-polish," are mirror-like. "Oiled" finishes are usually matte (not shiny). "Open-pore" finishes, common on some European pianos, are slightly "grainier" satin finishes due to the wood pores not being filled in prior to finishing. "Ebony" is a black finish.

Special-order–only styles and finishes are in italics.

Some descriptions of style and finish may be slightly different from the manufacturer's own for the purpose of clarity, consistency, saving space, or other reason.

Size

The height of a vertical piano is measured from the floor to the top of the piano. The length of a grand piano is measured from the very front (keyboard end) to the very back (tail end).

About Actual Selling or "Street" Prices

Buying a piano is something like buying a car—the list price is deliberately set high in anticipation of negotiating.[*] But sometimes this is carried to extremes, as when the salesperson reduces the price three times in the first fifteen minutes to barely half the sticker price. In situations like this, the customer, understandably confused, is bound to ask in exasperation, "What is the *real* price of this piano?"

---

[*] A relatively small number of dealers have non-negotiable prices.

Unfortunately, there *is* no "real" price. In theory, the dealer pays a wholesale price and then marks it up by an amount sufficient to cover the overhead and produce a profit. In practice, however, the markup can vary considerably from sale to sale depending on such factors as:

- how long the inventory has been sitting around, racking up finance charges for the dealer

- how much of a discount the dealer received at the wholesale level for buying in quantity or for paying cash

- the dealer's cash flow situation

- the competition in that particular geographic area for a particular brand or type of piano

- special piano sales events taking place in the area

- how the salesperson sizes up your situation and your willingness to pay

- the level of pre- and post-sale service the dealer seeks to provide

- the dealer's other overhead expenses

It's not unusual for one person to pay fifty percent more than another for the same brand and model of piano—sometimes even from the same dealer on the same day! It may seem as if pricing is so chaotic that no advice can be given, but in truth, enough piano sales do fall within a certain range of typical profit margins that some guidance is possible as long as the reader understands the limitations inherent in this kind of endeavor.

Historically, discounts from "standard" list price have averaged ten or fifteen percent in the piano business. In recent years, however, conditions have changed such that, according to some industry sources, the average discount from list has increased to twenty or twenty-five percent. Essentially, due to growing competition from used pianos and digital pianos, and a decrease in the cultural importance attached to having a piano in the home, there are too many dealers of new pianos chasing after too few consumer dollars.   In addition, higher labor costs worldwide and unfavorable international currency values make some brands so expensive in the U.S. that they can only be sold at very large discounts. I think, too, that consumers are becoming more savvy and are shopping around. Unfortunately, the overhead costs of running a traditional piano store are so high that most dealers cannot stay in business if they sell at an average discount from "standard" list price of more than about twenty percent. To survive, dealers are evolving multiple new approaches: becoming more efficient, instituting low-price/high volume strategies, cutting their overhead—sometimes including service—or subsidizing their meager sales of new pianos with used pianos (which command higher profit margins), rentals, rebuilding, and other products and services.

Although the average discount has increased, it is by no means uniform. Some brands dependably bring top dollar; others languish or the price is highly situational. I did consider giving a typical range of "street" prices for each brand and model listed in this volume, but concluded that the task would be too daunting due to the extreme variation that can exist from one situation to another, and because of the political fallout that would likely result from dealers and manufacturers who fear the loss of what little power they still have over aggressive, price-shopping customers. So, for now, I've decided just to give general advice in print. (For those who desire more specific information on "street" prices, I offer additional services, such as private telephone consultations and a Pricing Guide Service on the World Wide Web.)

It should be clearly understood that the advice given here is based on my own observations, subjective judgment, and general understanding of the piano market, *not* on statistical sales data or scientific analysis. (Brand-by-brand statistical sales data are virtually nonexistent.) This knowledge is the product of discussions with hundreds of customers, dealers, technicians, and industry executives over the years. Other industry observers may come to different conclusions. This rundown of "street" prices won't cover every brand, but should give a rough idea of what to expect and the ability to predict prices for some of the brands not specifically covered. I can't emphasize enough, however, that pricing can be highly situational, dependent on the mix of available products and the ease of comparison shopping in any particular geographic area, as well as on the financial situation of dealer and customer. The following generalizations should prove useful to you, but expect almost anything.

As a general rule of thumb:

- the more expensive the piano, the higher the possible discount

- the more "exclusive" a brand is perceived to be, the less likely head-to-head competition, and therefore the lower the possible discount

- the longer a piano remains unsold, the higher the possible discount

- the more service-intensive the piano, the lower the possible discount

Although discounts from "standard" list price for Japanese and Korean pianos typically start at perhaps fifteen percent, twenty or even thirty percent discounts are not uncommon in a moderately competitive environment, especially if the dealer knows the customer is shopping around. Korean pianos are disadvantaged by the presence in the market of too many different brand names made by the same two companies, driving prices down. Some Korean pianos are sold at large discounts (more than ten percent) from the published *wholesale* price to dealers who buy in quantity, a savings the dealers can pass on to the retail customers if they choose to do so. The problem for the consumer is that these wholesale discounts are not given out consistently among dealers, so figuring out an appropriate "street" price for a particular dealer and situation from the price information presented in this *Supplement* could be difficult.

The Boston piano, although manufactured in Japan, is generally viewed as being a little more "exclusive" due to its association with Steinway, so deep discounting is much less likely. Discounts in the range of ten to twenty percent are common. Baldwin, whose pianos are usually seen as being distinctly different from the Asian products even though they often share common price ranges, also benefits from exceptional name recognition and its historical "made in USA" connection. Discounting is likely to be moderate, in my experience—perhaps fifteen to twenty-five percent.

Western European instruments tend to be extremely expensive here due to their high quality, the high European cost of doing business, and unfavorable exchange rates. There appear to be two types of dealers of these pianos. One type, specializing in selling higher-quality instruments to a demanding clientele, manages to get top dollar for them despite their high price, with discounts averaging only twenty percent or so. They are not particularly into negotiating. The other type of dealer, probably more numerous, depends for his or her "bread and butter" on consumer-grade pianos and is pleased to make a relatively small profit on the occasional sale of a luxury instrument. Discounts here may well approach forty percent at times, especially if the piano has gone unsold for an extended period of time.

At the other end of the price spectrum, most Russian and Chinese pianos are so cheap, and require so much servicing by the dealer, that it's simply not cost-effective to sell them for much less than full list price. However, some dealers do use them as "loss leaders," that is, just to get people into the store, whereupon the customer is sold on a more expensive piano. In that situation, the occasional customer who actually chooses to buy the "leader" may do so at a large discount. Eastern European brands like Petrof are already seen as being a good deal for the money, have little in the way of direct competition, and are fairly service-intensive for the dealer, so expect moderate discounts— perhaps fifteen to twenty-five percent.

Steinway pianos have always been in a class by themselves, historically the only expensive piano to continually command high profit margins. Except for older Steinways and the occasional Mason & Hamlin, Steinway has little competition and fewer than one hundred dealers in the United States. Service requirements can be quite high, at least in part because of the higher standards often required to satisfy a fussier clientele. Historically, Steinway pianos have sold at or near full manufacturer's suggested retail price. (Some dealers even sell *above* suggested retail!) This is still true in many places, but in recent years I have seen a little more discounting than in the past. Ten to twenty percent is not unusual in some areas; as much as twenty-five percent would be rare.

There is no "fair" price for a piano except the one the buyer and seller agree on. The dealer is no more obligated to sell you a piano at a deep discount than you are obligated to pay the list price. Many dealers are simply not able to sell at the low end of the range consistently and still stay in business. It's understandable that you would like to pay the lowest price possible, and there's no harm in asking, but remember that piano shopping is not just about chasing the lowest price. Be sure you are getting the instrument that best suits your needs and preferences and that the dealer is committed to providing the proper pre- and post-sale service.

(Note: Remember that the "street" price discounts suggested above should be subtracted from the "standard" list prices in this *Supplement*, not from the manufacturer's suggested retail price.)

For more information on shopping for a new piano and on how to save money, please see pages 60–68 in *The Piano Book* (third edition).

Model	Size	Style and Finish	Price*

Astin-Weight

Verticals

Model	Size	Style and Finish	Price*
375	41"	Ebony	6,700.
375	41"	Santa Fe Oiled Oak	6,950.
375	41"	Spanish Oiled Oak	6,950.
375	41"	Spanish Lacquer Oak	6,950.
375	41"	Italian Oiled Walnut	7,120.
375	41"	Italian Lacquer Walnut	7,160.
375	41"	Regency Oiled Oak	7,120.
375	41"	Regency Lacquer Oak	7,200.
375	41"	Regency Oiled Walnut	7,200.
375	41"	Regency Lacquer Walnut	7,240.
U-500	50"	Ebony	9,950.
U-500	50"	Oiled Oak	9,950.
U-500	50"	Santa Fe Oiled Oak	9,950.
U-500	50"	Lacquer Oak	10,070.
U-500	50"	Oiled Walnut	10,270.
U-500	50"	Lacquer Walnut	10,350.

Grands

Model	Size	Style and Finish	Price*
———	5' 9"	Ebony	34,000.

August Förster — see "Förster, August"

Baldwin

Verticals

Model	Size	Style and Finish	Price*
660	43-1/2"	Georgian Mahogany	3,990.
662	43-1/2"	Queen Anne Regency Cherry	3,990.
665	43-1/2"	Transitional Country Oak	3,990.
667	43-1/2"	Country French Oak	3,990.
E100	43-1/2"	Continental Polished Ebony	4,190.
E100	43-1/2"	Continental Georgian Mahogany	3,990.
E100	43-1/2"	Continental Polished Ivory	4,190.
2090	43-1/2"	Hepplewhite Vintage Mahogany	4,590.
2095	43-1/2"	Regal Oak	4,590.
2096	43-1/2"	Queen Anne Royal Cherry	4,590.

*For explanation of terms and prices, please see pages 45–50.

Model	Size	Style and Finish	Price*

Baldwin (continued)

Model	Size	Style and Finish	Price*
243HPA	45"	Ebony	4,990.
243HPA	45"	Golden Oak	4,790.
243HPA	45"	American Walnut	4,990.
5050A	45"	Limited Edition Sheraton Mahogany	6,500.
5052A	45"	Limited Edition Queen Anne Cherry	6,500.
5057A	45"	Limited Edition Georgian Oak	6,500.
E250	45"	Contemporary Polished Ebony	5,190.
248A	48"	Polished Ebony	7,300.
248A	48"	American Walnut	7,100.
6000	52"	Ebony	9,300.
6000	52"	Mahogany	9,520.

Grands

Model	Size	Style and Finish	Price*
M	5' 2"	Ebony	21,900.
M	5' 2"	Polished Ebony	23,000.
M	5' 2"	Mahogany	22,640.
M	5' 2"	Polished Mahogany	23,500.
R	5' 8"	Ebony	24,800.
R	5' 8"	Polished Ebony	25,900.
R	5' 8"	Mahogany	26,000.
R	5' 8"	Polished Mahogany	26,900.
226	5' 8"	French Provincial Royal Cherry	30,800.
226	5' 8"	French Provincial Polished Cherry	31,700.
227	5' 8"	Louis XVI Mahogany	30,500.
L	6' 3"	Ebony	28,100.
L	6' 3"	Polished Ebony	29,200.
L	6' 3"	Mahogany	29,360.
L	6' 3"	Polished Mahogany	30,300.
SF10	7'	Ebony	42,100.
SF10	7'	Polished Ebony	43,200.
SF10	7'	Mahogany	43,500.
SD10	9'	Ebony	69,600.

ConcertMaster (approximate, including installation by factory or dealer)

Verticals	Playback only / with Perf. Option	7,640./8,928.
Grands	Playback only / with Perf. Option	9,200./10,500.
	With stop rail, add $300–$400	

Note: Discounts may apply, especially as an incentive to purchase the piano.

| --- | --- | --- | --- |

Bechstein, C.

Verticals

Model	Size	Style and Finish	Price*
Opus 112	44"	Ebony	18,380.
Opus 112	44"	Polished Ebony	19,360.
Opus 112	44"	Walnut	19,360.
Opus 112	44"	Polished Walnut	20,540.
Opus 112	44"	Mahogany	19,360.
Opus 112	44"	Polished Mahogany	20,540.
Opus 112	44"	Cherry	19,360.
Opus 112	44"	Polished Cherry	20,540.
Opus 112	44"	Oak	19,040.
Opus 112	44"	Polished Oak	20,540.
Opus 112	44"	Natural Oak/Ebony	19,040.
Opus 112	44"	Beech/Ebony	18,380.
Opus 112	44"	Polished White	20,540.
Opus 114	45"	Ebony	19,900.
Opus 114	45"	Polished Ebony	20,660.
Opus 114	45"	Walnut	20,660.
Opus 114	45"	Polished Walnut	21,400.
Opus 114	45"	Mahogany	20,660.
Opus 114	45"	Polished Mahogany	21,400.
Opus 114	45"	Cherry	20,660.
Opus 114	45"	Polished Cherry	21,400.
Opus 114	45"	Oak	20,660.
Opus 114	45"	Polished Oak	21,400.
Opus 114	45"	Natural Oak/Ebony	20,660.
Opus 114	45"	Polished White	21,400.
Studio 118	47"	Polished Ebony	23,780.
Studio 118	47"	Walnut	23,780.
Studio 118	47"	Polished Walnut	25,080.
Studio 118	47"	Mahogany	23,780.
Studio 118	47"	Polished Mahogany	25,080.
Studio 118	47"	Cherry	23,780.
Studio 118	47"	Polished Cherry	25,080.
Studio 118	47"	Oak	23,780.
Studio 118	47"	Polished Oak	25,080.

*For explanation of terms and prices, please see pages 45–50.

Model	Size	Style and Finish	Price*
Bechstein, C. (continued)			
Studio 118	47"	Polished White	25,080.
Studio 122	48"	Polished Ebony	25,740.
Studio 122	48"	Walnut	25,740.
Studio 122	48"	Polished Walnut	26,920.
Studio 122	48"	Mahogany	25,740.
Studio 122	48"	Polished Mahogany	26,920.
Studio 122	48"	Cherry	25,740.
Studio 122	48"	Polished Cherry	26,920.
Studio 122	48"	Oak	25,740.
Studio 122	48"	Polished Oak	26,920.
Studio 122	48"	Polished White	26,920.
Studio 122	48"	"Elegance" Polished Ebony	26,600.
Studio 122	48"	"Elegance" Walnut	26,600.
Studio 122	48"	"Elegance" Polished Walnut	29,400.
Studio 122	48"	"Elegance" Mahogany	26,600.
Studio 122	48"	"Elegance" Polished Mahogany	29,400.
Studio 122	48"	"Elegance" Cherry	26,600.
Studio 122	48"	"Elegance" Polished Cherry	29,400.
Studio 122	48"	"Elegance" Polished White	29,400.
11A	50"	Polished Ebony	37,600.
11A	50"	Walnut	37,600.
11A	50"	Polished Walnut	38,500.
11A	50"	Mahogany	36,740.
11A	50"	Polished Mahogany	38,500.
11A	50"	Cherry	37,600.
11A	50"	Polished Cherry	38,500.
11A	50"	Oak	36,740.
11A	50"	Polished Oak	38,500.
11A	50"	Polished White	38,500.
8A	52"	Polished Ebony	40,940.
8A	52"	Walnut	40,940.
8A	52"	Polished Walnut	41,620.
8A	52"	Mahogany	40,700.
8A	52"	Polished Mahogany	41,620.
8A	52"	Cherry	40,940.
8A	52"	Polished Cherry	41,620.

Model	Size	Style and Finish	Price*
8A	52"	Oak	40,700.
8A	52"	Polished Oak	41,620.
8A	52"	Polished White	41,620.
8A	52"	*Add for sostenuto*	1,060.

Grands

Model	Size	Style and Finish	Price*
K-158	5' 2"	Polished Ebony	73,840.
K-158	5' 2"	Mahogany	71,280.
K-158	5' 2"	Oak	71,280.
K-158	5' 2"	Walnut	73,840.
K-158	5' 2"	Cherry	73,840.
K-158	5' 2"	Polished Woods (above)	75,700.
K-158	5' 2"	Polished White	75,700.
K-158	5' 2"	Yew	75,700.
K-158	5' 2"	Classic or Chippendale Pol. Ebony	82,420.
K-158	5' 2"	Classic or Chippendale Mahogany	79,880.
K-158	5' 2"	Classic or Chippendale Oak	79,980.
K-158	5' 2"	Classic or Chippendale Walnut	82,420.
K-158	5' 2"	Classic or Chippendale Cherry	82,420.
K-158	5' 2"	Classic or Chip. Pol. Woods (above)	84,260.
K-158	5' 2"	Classic or Chippendale Polished White	84,260.
K-158	5' 2"	Classic or Chippendale Yew	84,260.
M-180	5' 11"	Polished Ebony	80,700.
M-180	5' 11"	Mahogany	78,600.
M-180	5' 11"	Oak	78,600.
M-180	5' 11"	Walnut	80,700.
M-180	5' 11"	Cherry	80,700.
M-180	5' 11"	Polished Woods (above)	83,140.
M-180	5' 11"	Yew	83,140.
M-180	5' 11"	Polished White	83,140.
M-180	5' 11"	Polished Pyramid Mahogany	91,860.
M-180	5' 11"	Burled Walnut	91,860.
M-180	5' 11"	Polished Varvona	94,660.
M-180	5' 11"	Polished Moabi	94,660.
M-180	5' 11"	Polished Mahogany with Inlays	107,680.
M-180	5' 11"	Classic or Chippendale Pol. Ebony	90,700.
M-180	5' 11"	Classic or Chippendale Mahogany	88,380.
M-180	5' 11"	Classic or Chippendale Oak	88,380.

*For explanation of terms and prices, please see pages 45–50.

Model	Size	Style and Finish	Price*
Bechstein, C. (continued)			
M-180	5' 11"	Classic or Chippendale Walnut	90,700.
M-180	5' 11"	Classic or Chippendale Cherry	90,700.
M-180	5' 11"	Classic or Chip. Pol. Woods (above)	93,020.
M-180	5' 11"	Classic or Chippendale Polished White	93,020.
M-180	5' 11"	Classic or Chippendale Burled Walnut	101,460.
M-180	5' 11"	Classic or Chippendale Pol. Varvona	104,080.
M-180	5' 11"	Classic or Chippendale Polished Moabi	104,080.
A-189	6' 2"	Ebony	60,460.
A-189	6' 2"	Polished Ebony	65,240.
A-189	6' 2"	Mahogany	63,500.
A-189	6' 2"	Oak	63,500.
A-189	6' 2"	Walnut	65,240.
A-189	6' 2"	Cherry	65,240.
A-189	6' 2"	Polished Woods (above)	67,900.
A-189	6' 2"	Polished White	67,900.
A-189	6' 2"	Polished Pyramid Mahogany	77,260.
A-189	6' 2"	Polished Varvona	79,960.
A-189	6' 2"	Polished Moabi	79,960.
A-189	6' 2"	Classic Polished Ebony	74,780.
A-189	6' 2"	Classic Mahogany	73,020.
A-189	6' 2"	Classic Oak	73,020.
A-189	6' 2"	Classic Walnut	74,780.
A-189	6' 2"	Classic Cherry	74,780.
A-189	6' 2"	Classic Polished Woods (above)	77,440.
A-189	6' 2"	Classic Polished White	77,440.
A-189	6' 2"	Classic Burled Walnut	85,120.
A-189	6' 2"	Classic Polished Varvona	87,900.
A-189	6' 2"	Classic Polished Moabi	87,900.
B-208	6' 10"	Polished Ebony	90,700.
B-208	6' 10"	Mahogany	89,540.
B-208	6' 10"	Oak	89,540.
B-208	6' 10"	Walnut	90,700.
B-208	6' 10"	Cherry	90,700.
B-208	6' 10"	Polished Woods (above)	95,000.
B-208	6' 10"	Classic Polished Ebony	101,640.
B-208	6' 10"	Classic Mahogany	99,800.

Model	Size	Style and Finish	Price*
B-208	6' 10"	Classic Oak	99,800.
B-208	6' 10"	Classic Walnut	101,640.
B-208	6' 10"	Classic Cherry	101,640.
B-208	6' 10"	Classic Polished Woods (above)	104,660.
C-232	7' 6"	Polished Ebony	111,160.
C-232	7' 6"	Classic Polished Ebony	120,460.
EN-280	9' 2"	Polished Ebony	142,560.

Bentley

Prices are FOB England and do not include duty, freight, and other costs of importing. Oak, ash, and cherry are available at the same price as mahogany. Polished white is available at the same price as polished ebony.

Verticals

Model	Size	Style and Finish	Price
Concord	43"	Polished Ebony	8,900.
Concord	43"	Mahogany	7,560.
Concord	43"	Polished Mahogany	8,900.
Concord	43"	Walnut	7,560.
Concord	43"	Polished Walnut	8,900.
Concord	43"	Teak	7,560.
Concord	43"	Chippendale Mahogany	7,920.
Concord	43"	Chippendale Polished Mahogany	9,500.
Concord	43"	Chippendale Walnut	7,920.
Concord	43"	Chippendale Polished Walnut	9,500.
Heritage	43"	Mahogany	8,160.
Heritage	43"	Polished Mahogany	9,320.
Wessex	46"	Polished Ebony	9,320.
Wessex	46"	Mahogany	8,160.
Wessex	46"	Polished Mahogany	9,320.
Wessex	46"	Walnut	8,160.
Wessex	46"	Polished Walnut	9,320.
Berkeley	46"	Mahogany	8,920.
Berkeley	46"	Polished Mahogany	10,240.
Exeter	47"	Polished Ebony	10,260.
Exeter	47"	Mahogany	9,040.
Exeter	47"	Polished Mahogany	10,260.
Exeter	47"	Walnut	9,040.
Exeter	47"	Polished Walnut	10,260.

*For explanation of terms and prices, please see pages 45–50.

Model	Size	Style and Finish	Price*

Bentley (continued)

Model	Size	Style and Finish	Price*
Berlin	47"	Polished Ebony	10,440.
Berlin	47"	Mahogany	9,400.
Berlin	47"	Polished Mahogany	10,440.
Berlin	47"	Walnut	9,400.
Berlin	47"	Polished Walnut	10,440.
London	47"	Mahogany	9,840.
London	47"	Polished Mahogany	10,940.
Belgrave	47"	Mahogany	9,840.
Belgrave	47"	Polished Mahogany	10,940.
Chelsea	47"	Mahogany	9,840.
Chelsea	47"	Polished Mahogany	10,940.
Salisbury	47"	Mahogany	9,880.
Salisbury	47"	Polished Mahogany	10,980.
Salisbury	47"	Walnut	9,880.
Salisbury	47"	Polished Walnut	10,980.
Esher	47"	Mahogany	10,220.
Esher	47"	Polished Mahogany	11,380.
Esher	47"	Walnut	10,220.
Esher	47"	Polished Walnut	11,380.

Bergmann

Verticals

Model	Size	Style and Finish	Price*
ER-109	43"	Continental Polished Ebony	2,390.
ER-109	43"	Continental Polished Red Mahogany	2,500.
ER-121	48"	Polished Ebony	2,990.
ER-121	48"	Polished Red Mahogany	3,100.

Blondel, G.

Verticals

Model	Size	Style and Finish	Price*
Bolero	43"	Ebony	6,680.
Bolero	43"	Polished Ebony	6,780.
Bolero	43"	Mahogany	6,680.
Bolero	43"	Polished Mahogany	6,780.
Bolero	43"	Walnut	6,680.
Bolero	43"	Polished Walnut	6,780.

Model	Size	Style and Finish	Price*
Bolero	43"	Oak	6,680.
Bolero	43"	Polished Oak	6,780.
Sarabande	47"	Ebony	7,680.
Sarabande	47"	Polished Ebony	7,780.
Sarabande	47"	Mahogany	7,680.
Sarabande	47"	Polished Mahogany	7,780.
Sarabande	47"	Walnut	7,680.
Sarabande	47"	Polished Walnut	7,780.
Sarabande	47"	Oak	7,680.
Sarabande	47"	Polished Oak	7,780.
Grands			
Tocata	6' 1"	Ebony	23,680.
Tocata	6' 1"	Polished Ebony	23,780.
Tocata	6' 1"	Mahogany	23,680.
Tocata	6' 1"	Polished Mahogany	23,780.
Tocata	6' 1"	Walnut	23,680.
Tocata	6' 1"	Polished Walnut	23,780.
Tocata	6' 1"	Oak	23,680.
Tocata	6' 1"	Polished Oak	23,780.

Blüthner

Verticals			
I	46"	Ebony	16,118.
I	46"	Polished Ebony	17,316.
I	46"	Walnut	17,522.
I	46"	Polished Walnut	19,026.
I	46"	Open-Pore Walnut	16,656.
I	46"	Mahogany	16,754.
I	46"	Polished Mahogany	18,000.
I	46"	Cherry	16,754.
I	46"	Polished Cherry	18,000.
I	46"	Polished White	18,000.
A	48"	Ebony	20,620.
A	48"	Polished Ebony	22,158.
A	48"	Walnut	22,420.
A	48"	Polished Walnut	24,354.

*For explanation of terms and prices, please see pages 45–50.

Model	Size	Style and Finish	Price*
Blüthner (continued)			
A	48"	Open-Pore Walnut	21,310.
A	48"	Mahogany	21,436.
A	48"	Polished Mahogany	23,036.
A	48"	Cherry	21,436.
A	48"	Polished Cherry	23,036.
A	48"	Polished White	23,036.
B	52"	Ebony	22,782.
B	52"	Polished Ebony	24,482.
B	52"	Walnut	24,772.
B	52"	Polished Walnut	26,910.
B	52"	Open-Pore Walnut	23,546.
B	52"	Mahogany	23,686.
B	52"	Polished Mahogany	25,454.
B	52"	Cherry	23,686.
B	52"	Polished Cherry	25,454.
B	52"	Polished White	25,454.
Grands			
11	5'	Ebony	40,688.
11	5'	Polished Ebony	43,734.
11	5'	Walnut	44,258.
11	5'	Polished Walnut	48,086.
11	5'	Open-Pore Walnut	42,054.
11	5'	Mahogany	42,308.
11	5'	Polished Mahogany	45,476.
11	5'	Cherry	42,308.
11	5'	Polished Cherry	45,476.
11	5'	Polished White	45,476.
11	5'	"Saxony" Polished Pyramid Mahogany	56,794.
11	5'	"Saxony" Polished Burl Walnut Inlay	56,794.
11	5'	French Baroque Dark Walnut	58,970.
11	5'	French Baroque White	70,726.
11	5'	Classic Victorian Polished Ebony	50,266.
11	5'	Classic Victorian Polished Mahogany	52,268.
11	5'	Classic Victorian Polished Cherry	52,268.
11	5'	Classic Alexandra Polished Ebony	50,266.

Model	Size	Style and Finish	Price*
11	5'	Classic Alexandra Polished Mahogany	52,268.
11	5'	Classic Alexandra Polished Cherry	52,268.
10	5' 5"	Ebony	45,640.
10	5' 5"	Polished Ebony	49,062.
10	5' 5"	Walnut	49,650.
10	5' 5"	Polished Walnut	53,948.
10	5' 5"	Open-Pore Walnut	47,176.
10	5' 5"	Mahogany	47,460.
10	5' 5"	Polished Mahogany	51,018.
10	5' 5"	Cherry	47,460.
10	5' 5"	Polished Cherry	51,018.
10	5' 5"	Polished Bubinga	51,018.
10	5' 5"	Polished White	51,018.
10	5' 5"	"Saxony" Polished Pyramid Mahogany	63,720.
10	5' 5"	"Saxony" Polished Burl Walnut Inlay	63,720.
10	5' 5"	French Baroque Dark Walnut	66,164.
10	5' 5"	French Baroque White	79,358.
10	5' 5"	Classic Victorian Polished Ebony	56,392.
10	5' 5"	Classic Victorian Polished Mahogany	58,638.
10	5' 5"	Classic Victorian Polished Cherry	58,638.
10	5' 5"	Classic Alexandra Polished Ebony	56,392.
10	5' 5"	Classic Alexandra Polished Mahogany	58,638.
10	5' 5"	Classic Alexandra Polished Cherry	58,638.
10	5' 5"	Special Design Polished Rosewood	66,164.
6	6' 2"	Ebony	51,248.
6	6' 2"	Polished Ebony	55,092.
6	6' 2"	Walnut	55,802.
6	6' 2"	Polished Walnut	60,580.
6	6' 2"	Open-Pore Walnut	52,972.
6	6' 2"	Mahogany	53,292.
6	6' 2"	Polished Mahogany	57,286.
6	6' 2"	Cherry	53,292.
6	6' 2"	Polished Cherry	57,286.
6	6' 2"	Polished Bubinga	57,286.
6	6' 2"	Polished White	57,286.
6	6' 2"	"Saxony" Polished Pyramid Mahogany	71,560.
6	6' 2"	"Saxony" Polished Burl Walnut Inlay	71,560.

*For explanation of terms and prices, please see pages 45–50.

Model	Size	Style and Finish	Price*
		Blüthner (continued)	
6	6' 2"	French Baroque Dark Walnut	74,302.
6	6' 2"	French Baroque White	89,122.
6	6' 2"	Classic Victorian Polished Ebony	63,326.
6	6' 2"	Classic Victorian Polished Mahogany	65,850.
6	6' 2"	Classic Victorian Polished Cherry	65,850.
6	6' 2"	Classic Alexandra Polished Ebony	63,326.
6	6' 2"	Classic Alexandra Polished Mahogany	65,850.
6	6' 2"	Classic Alexandra Polished Cherry	65,850.
6	6' 2"	Special Design Polished Rosewood	74,302.
4	6' 10"	Ebony	57,610.
4	6' 10"	Polished Ebony	61,932.
4	6' 10"	Walnut	62,672.
4	6' 10"	Polished Walnut	68,104.
4	6' 10"	Open-Pore Walnut	62,672.
4	6' 10"	Mahogany	59,906.
4	6' 10"	Polished Mahogany	64,402.
4	6' 10"	Cherry	59,906.
4	6' 10"	Polished Cherry	64,402.
4	6' 10"	Polished Bubinga	64,402.
4	6' 10"	Polished White	64,402.
4	6' 10"	"Saxony" Polished Pyramid Mahogany	80,452.
4	6' 10"	"Saxony" Polished Burl Walnut Inlay	80,452.
4	6' 10"	Classic Victorian Polished Ebony	71,190.
4	6' 10"	Classic Victorian Polished Mahogany	74,032.
4	6' 10"	Classic Victorian Polished Cherry	74,032.
4	6' 10"	Classic Alexandra Polished Ebony	71,190.
4	6' 10"	Classic Alexandra Polished Mahogany	74,032.
4	6' 10"	Classic Alexandra Polished Cherry	74,032.
4	6' 10"	Special Design Polished Rosewood	83,020.
2	7' 6"	Ebony	64,576.
2	7' 6"	Polished Ebony	69,422.
2	7' 6"	Polished White	72,114.
2	7' 6"	Special Design Polished Rosewood	93,090.
1	9' 2"	Ebony	73,000.
1	9' 2"	Polished Ebony	78,466.
1	9' 2"	Polished White	81,588.

Bohemia / Rieger-Kloss

All pianos bear the Rieger-Kloss name except the 7' grand, which bears the Bohemia name.

Verticals

Model	Size	Style and Finish	Price*
R-109	43"	Continental Polished Ebony	4,690.
R-109	43"	Continental Walnut	4,690.
R-109	43"	Continental Polished Walnut	4,690.
R-109	43"	Continental Polished Mahogany	4,690.
R-109	43"	Continental Light Oak	4,690.
R-111	44"	Continental Ebony	3,990.
R-111	44"	Continental Rustic Oak	3,990.
R-111	44"	Continental Light Beech	3,990.
R-111	44"	Continental Light Walnut	3,990.
R-118	47"	Continental Polished Ebony	4,990.
R-118	47"	Continental Walnut	4,990.
R-118	47"	Continental Cherry	4,990.
R-118	47"	Continental Light Oak	4,990.
R-121	48"	Polished Ebony	5,190.
R-122	48"	Demi-Chippendale Polished Walnut	5,790.
R-122	48"	Demi-Chippendale Polished Mahogany	5,790.
R-123	48"	Polished Ebony	5,590.
R-123	48"	Polished Walnut	5,590.
R-123	48"	Polished Mahogany	5,590.
R-123	48"	Light Oak	5,590.
R-125	50"	Polished Ebony	6,990.
R-126	50"	Polished Ebony	6,190.

Grands

Model	Size	Style and Finish	Price*
RG-158	5' 2"	Polished Ebony	18,990.
RG-158	5' 2"	Polished Walnut	19,390.
RG-158	5' 2"	Polished Mahogany	19,390.
RG-185	6' 1"	Polished Ebony	21,900.
RG-185	6' 1"	Polished Walnut	22,590.
RG-185	6' 1"	Polished Mahogany	22,590.
RG-185	6' 1"	Polished White	21,990.
BG-214	7'	"Bohemia" Polished Ebony	31,200.

*For explanation of terms and prices, please see pages 45–50.

Model	Size	Style and Finish	Price*

Bösendorfer

Prices do not include bench.

Verticals

Model	Size	Style and Finish	Price
130	52"	Polished Ebony	36,980.
130	52"	Walnut	39,980.
130	52"	Polished Walnut	39,980.
130	52"	Open-Pore Walnut	39,980.
130	52"	Mahogany	39,980.
130	52"	Polished Mahogany	39,980.
130	52"	Open-Pore Mahogany	39,980.
130	52"	Polished Pommelé Mahogany	39,980.
130	52"	Polished Pyramid Mahogany	41,980.
130	52"	Polished Bird's-Eye Maple	41,980.
130	52"	Rosewood	41,980.
130	52"	White	39,980.
130	52"	Polished White	39,980.

Grands

Model	Size	Style and Finish	Price
170	5' 8"	Polished Ebony	71,980.
170	5' 8"	Walnut	75,980.
170	5' 8"	Polished Walnut	75,980.
170	5' 8"	Open-Pore Walnut	75,980.
170	5' 8"	Mahogany	75,980.
170	5' 8"	Polished Mahogany	75,980.
170	5' 8"	Open-Pore Mahogany	75,980.
170	5' 8"	Polished Pommelé Mahogany	75,980.
170	5' 8"	Polished Pyramid Mahogany	80,780.
170	5' 8"	Polished Bird's-Eye Maple	80,780.
170	5' 8"	Rosewood	80,780.
170	5' 8"	White	75,980.
170	5' 8"	Polished White	75,980.
170	5' 8"	"Johann Strauss" Polished Ebony	76,980.
170	5' 8"	"Franz Schubert" Polished Cherry	87,980.
170	5' 8"	"Senator" Polished Mahogany	89,380.
170	5' 8"	"Academy" Ebony	65,980.
170	5' 8"	"Hollein," "Baroque," Chippendale	on request
200	6' 7"	Polished Ebony	83,980.
200	6' 7"	Walnut	91,180.

Model	Size	Style and Finish	Price*
200	6' 7"	Polished Walnut	91,180.
200	6' 7"	Open-Pore Walnut	91,180.
200	6' 7"	Mahogany	91,180.
200	6' 7"	Polished Mahogany	91,180.
200	6' 7"	Open-Pore Mahogany	91,180.
200	6' 7"	Polished Pommelé Mahogany	91,980.
200	6' 7"	Polished Pyramid Mahogany	95,580.
200	6' 7"	Polished Bird's-Eye Maple	95,580.
200	6' 7"	Rosewood	95,580.
200	6' 7"	White	91,180.
200	6' 7"	Polished White	91,180.
200	6' 7"	"Johann Strauss" Polished Ebony	88,980.
200	6' 7"	"Franz Schubert" Polished Cherry	100,380.
200	6' 7"	"Senator" Polished Mahogany	97,380.
200	6' 7"	"Academy" Ebony	73,980.
200	6' 7"	"Hollein," "Baroque," Chippendale	on request
214	7'	Polished Ebony	97,980.
214	7'	Walnut	103,980.
214	7'	Polished Walnut	103,980.
214	7'	Open-Pore Walnut	103,980.
214	7'	Mahogany	103,980.
214	7'	Polished Mahogany	103,980.
214	7'	Open-Pore Mahogany	103,980.
214	7'	Polished Pommelé Mahogany	103,980.
214	7'	Polished Pyramid Mahogany	107,580.
214	7'	Polished Bird's-Eye Maple	107,580.
214	7'	Rosewood	107,580.
214	7'	White	103,980.
214	7'	Polished White	103,980.
214	7'	"Johann Strauss" Polished Ebony	100,980.
214	7'	"Franz Schubert" Polished Cherry	111,980.
214	7'	"Senator" Polished Mahogany	109,980.
214	7'	"Academy" Ebony	87,180.
214	7'	"Hollein," "Baroque," Chippendale	on request
225	7' 4"	Polished Ebony	103,980.
225	7' 4"	Walnut	112,780.
225	7' 4"	Polished Walnut	112,780.

*For explanation of terms and prices, please see pages 45–50.

Model	Size	Style and Finish	Price*

Bösendorfer (continued)

Model	Size	Style and Finish	Price*
225	7' 4"	Open-Pore Walnut	112,780.
225	7' 4"	Mahogany	112,780.
225	7' 4"	Polished Mahogany	112,780.
225	7' 4"	Open-Pore Mahogany	112,780.
225	7' 4"	Polished Pommelé Mahogany	112,780.
225	7' 4"	Polished Pyramid Mahogany	117,580.
225	7' 4"	Polished Bird's-Eye Maple	117,580.
225	7' 4"	Rosewood	117,580.
225	7' 4"	White	112,780.
225	7' 4"	Polished White	112,780.
225	7' 4"	"Johann Strauss" Polished Ebony	108,980.
225	7' 4"	"Franz Schubert" Polished Cherry	123,580.
225	7' 4"	"Senator" Polished Mahogany	119,380.
225	7' 4"	"Academy" Ebony	93,980.
225	7' 4"	"Hollein," "Baroque," Chippendale	on request
275	9'	Polished Ebony	131,980.
275	9'	All other styles and finishes listed above,	on request
275	9' 6"	Polished Ebony	159,980.
290	9' 6"	All other styles and finishes listed above,	on request

Boston

Verticals

Model	Size	Style and Finish	Price*
UP-118C	45"	Continental Polished Ebony	7,100.
UP-118C	45"	Continental Polished Walnut	7,740.
UP-118C	45"	Continental Polished Mahogany	7,740.
UP-118C	45"	Continental Polished White	7,530.
UP-118E	46"	Polished Ebony	7,530.
UP-118E	46"	Walnut	8,390.
UP-118E	46"	Polished Walnut	8,590.
UP-118E	46"	Polished Mahogany	8,590.
UP-118E	46"	Polished White	8,390.
UP-118S	46"	Open-Pore Honey Oak	5,690.
UP-118S	46"	Open-Pore Black Oak	5,690.
UP-118S	46"	Open-Pore Red Oak	5,690.
UP-125E	49"	Polished Ebony	8,500.

Model	Size	Style and Finish	Price*
UP-125E	49"	Polished Mahogany	9,790.
UP-132E	52"	Polished Ebony	10,300.
Grands			
GP-156	5' 1"	Ebony	13,980.
GP-156	5' 1"	Polished Ebony	13,980.
GP-163	5' 4"	Ebony	16,780.
GP-163	5' 4"	Polished Ebony	17,180.
GP-163	5' 4"	Mahogany	18,280.
GP-163	5' 4"	Polished Mahogany	18,720.
GP-163	5' 4"	Walnut	18,500.
GP-163	5' 4"	Polished Walnut	18,940.
GP-163	5' 4"	Polished White	17,640.
GP-163	5' 4"	Polished Ivory	17,640.
GP-178	5' 10"	Ebony	19,360.
GP-178	5' 10"	Polished Ebony	19,780.
GP-178	5' 10"	Mahogany	20,660.
GP-178	5' 10"	Polished Mahogany	21,080.
GP-178	5' 10"	Walnut	20,880.
GP-178	5' 10"	Polished Walnut	21,520.
GP-178	5' 10"	Polished White	20,220.
GP-178	5' 10"	Polished Ivory	20,220.
GP-193	6' 4"	Ebony	24,540.
GP-193	6' 4"	Polished Ebony	25,180.
GP-193	6' 4"	Walnut	27,340.
GP-193	6' 4"	Polished Mahogany	27,540.
GP-193	6' 4"	Polished White	26,480.
GP-218	7' 2"	Ebony	31,180.
GP-218	7' 2"	Polished Ebony	31,980.

Brentwood

Verticals			
MP005	42"	Continental Polished Ebony	2,590.
MP005	42"	Continental Polished Cherry	2,590.
MP005	42"	Continental Polished Dark Walnut	2,590.
MP005	42"	Continental Polished White	2,790.
MP012	46"	Polished Ebony	2,990.

*For explanation of terms and prices, please see pages 45–50.

Model	Size	Style and Finish	Price*

Brentwood (continued)

Model	Size	Style and Finish	Price
MP012	46"	Polished Cherry	2,990.
MP012	46"	Polished Dark Walnut	2,990.
MP012	46"	Polished White	3,090.
MP012C	46"	Polished Ebony	2,990.
MP012C	46"	Polished Cherry	2,990.
MP012C	46"	Polished Dark Walnut	2,990.
MP012C	46"	Polished White	3,090.

Broadwood, John, & Sons

Prices are FOB England and do not include duty, freight, and other costs of importing. Oak, ash, and cherry are available at the same price as mahogany. Polished white is available at the same price as polished ebony.

Verticals

Model	Size	Style and Finish	Price
St. James	44"	Polished Ebony	9,560.
St. James	44"	Mahogany	8,340.
St. James	44"	Polished Mahogany	9,560.
St. James	44"	Walnut	8,340.
St. James	44"	Polished Walnut	9,560.
Berwick	47"	Polished Ebony	11,000.
Berwick	47"	Mahogany	9,580.
Berwick	47"	Polished Mahogany	11,000.
Berwick	47"	Walnut	9,580.
Berwick	47"	Polished Walnut	11,000.
Imperial	47"	Mahogany	10,960.
Imperial	47"	Polished Mahogany	12,180.
Stratford	50"	Polished Ebony	15,150.
Stratford	50"	Mahogany	13,960.
Stratford	50"	Polished Mahogany	15,150.
Stratford	50"	Walnut	13,960.
Stratford	50"	Polished Walnut	15,150.

Grands

Model	Size	Style and Finish	Price
Boudoir	6'	Polished Ebony	40,820.

Charles R. Walter — see "Walter, Charles R."

Model	Size	Style and Finish	Price*

Chickering

Grands

Model	Size	Style and Finish	Price*
410D	4' 10"	Ebony	13,180.
410D	4' 10"	Polished Ebony	13,700.
410D	4' 10"	Mahogany	13,940.
410D	4' 10"	Polished Mahogany	14,500.
410DQA	4' 10"	Queen Anne Royal Cherry	15,700.
410DQA	4' 10"	Queen Anne Polished Cherry	16,300.
410DFP	4' 10"	French Provincial Royal Cherry	16,330.
507D	5' 7"	Ebony	15,980.
507D	5' 7"	Polished Ebony	16,640.
507D	5' 7"	Mahogany	17,040.
507D	5' 7"	Polished Mahogany	17,760.
507DDL	5' 7"	Sheraton-Hepplewhite Mahogany	18,350.
507DCD	5' 7"	Chippendale Royal Cherry	18,920.

Estonia

Grands

Model	Size	Style and Finish	Price*
163	5' 4"	Ebony	17,940.
163	5' 4"	Polished Ebony	17,940.
163	5' 4"	Bubinga	19,734.
163	5' 4"	Polished Bubinga	19,734.
163	5' 4"	Bubinga Pommele	19,734.
163	5' 4"	Polished Bubinga Pommele	19,734.
163	5' 4"	African Makore	19,734.
163	5' 4"	Polished African Makore	19,734.
163	5' 4"	American Walnut	19,734.
163	5' 4"	Polished American Walnut	19,734.
163	5' 4"	*White*	19,734.
163	5' 4"	*Polished White*	19,734.
168	5' 6"	Ebony	19,140.
168	5' 6"	Polished Ebony	19,140.
168	5' 6"	Bubinga	21,054.
168	5' 6"	Polished Bubinga	21,054.
168	5' 6"	Bubinga Pommele	21,054.
168	5' 6"	Polished Bubinga Pommele	21,054.

*For explanation of terms and prices, please see pages 45–50.

Model	Size	Style and Finish	Price*

Estonia (continued)

168	5' 6"	African Makore	21,054.
168	5' 6"	Polished African Makore	21,054.
168	5' 6"	American Walnut	21,054.
168	5' 6"	Polished American Walnut	21,054.
168	5' 6"	*White*	21,054.
168	5' 6"	*Polished White*	21,054.
190	6' 3"	Ebony	22,740.
190	6' 3"	Polished Ebony	22,740.
190	6' 3"	*White*	25,014.
190	6' 3"	*Polished White*	25,014.
190	6' 3"	*Chippendale Ebony*	24,740.
190	6' 3"	*Chippendale Polished Ebony*	24,740.
190	6' 3"	*Chippendale White*	27,214.
190	6' 3"	*Chippendale Polished White*	27,214.
273	9'	Ebony	40,940.
273	9'	Polished Ebony	40,940.
273	9'	*White*	45,034.
273	9'	*Polished White*	45,034.

Eterna

Verticals

ERC 10	44"	Continental Polished Ebony	3,390.

Everett

Verticals

EV-43	43"	Continental Polished Ebony	2,700.
EV-43	43"	Continental Polished Mahogany	2,780.
EV-45	45"	Polished Ebony	3,300.
EV-45	45"	Polished Mahogany	3,380.
EV-45 S	45"	Chippendale Polished Ebony	3,700.
EV-45 S	45"	Chippendale Polished Mahogany	3,780.

Grands

EV-540	5' 4"	Polished Ebony	10,390.

Fazioli

Fazioli is willing to make custom-designed cases with exotic veneers, marquetry, and other embellishments. Prices on request to Fazioli.

Grands

Model	Size	Style and Finish	Price*
F156	5' 2"	Ebony	69,800.
F156	5' 2"	Polished Ebony	71,300.
F156	5' 2"	Walnut	74,100.
F156	5' 2"	Polished Walnut	76,500.
F156	5' 2"	Polished Pyramid Mahogany	78,800.
F156	5' 2"	Cherry	74,100.
F156	5' 2"	Polished Cherry	76,500.
F183	6'	Ebony	77,700.
F183	6'	Polished Ebony	79,300.
F183	6'	Walnut	83,100.
F183	6'	Polished Walnut	85,100.
F183	6'	Polished Pyramid Mahogany	88,200.
F183	6'	Cherry	83,100.
F183	6'	Polished Cherry	85,100.
F212	6' 11"	Ebony	87,400.
F212	6' 11"	Polished Ebony	89,500.
F212	6' 11"	Walnut	93,400.
F212	6' 11"	Polished Walnut	95,900.
F212	6' 11"	Polished Pyramid Mahogany	99,200.
F212	6' 11"	Cherry	93,400.
F212	6' 11"	Polished Cherry	95,900.
F228	7' 6"	Ebony	98,500.
F228	7' 6"	Polished Ebony	100,700.
F228	7' 6"	Walnut	104,700.
F228	7' 6"	Polished Walnut	107,100.
F228	7' 6"	Polished Pyramid Mahogany	112,100.
F228	7' 6"	Cherry	104,700.
F228	7' 6"	Polished Cherry	107,100.
F278	9' 2"	Ebony	126,900.
F278	9' 2"	Polished Ebony	129,200.
F278	9' 2"	Walnut	134,600.
F278	9' 2"	Polished Walnut	138,700.
F278	9' 2"	Polished Pyramid Mahogany	143,500.

*For explanation of terms and prices, please see pages 45–50.

Model	Size	Style and Finish	Price*

Fazioli (continued)

Model	Size	Style and Finish	Price*
F278	9' 2"	Cherry	134,600.
F278	9' 2"	Polished Cherry	138,700.
F308	10' 2"	Ebony	165,900.
F308	10' 2"	Polished Ebony	168,300.
F308	10' 2"	Walnut	175,500.
F308	10' 2"	Polished Walnut	177,800.
F308	10' 2"	Polished Pyramid Mahogany	183,300.
F308	10' 2"	Cherry	175,500.
F308	10' 2"	Polished Cherry	177,800.

Förster, August

Verticals

Model	Size	Style and Finish	Price*
116C	46"	Chippendale Polished Ebony	17,800.
116C	46"	Chippendale Polished Walnut	17,800.
116E	46"	Polished Ebony	17,800.
116	46"	Polished White	18,800.
125G	50"	Polished Ebony	21,600.
125	50"	Polished White	22,600.

Grands

Model	Size	Style and Finish	Price*
170	5' 7"	Polished Ebony	37,000.
170	5' 7"	Polished Walnut	37,000.
170	5' 7"	Polished Mahogany	37,000.
170	5' 7"	Polished White	38,960.
170	5' 7"	Chippendale	45,000.
170	5' 7"	Antique	on request
170	5' 7"	Rococo	on request
190	6' 4"	Polished Ebony	42,000.
190	6' 4"	Polished Walnut	42,000.
190	6' 4"	Polished Mahogany	42,000.
190	6' 4"	Polished White	43,960.
190	6' 4"	Chippendale	50,000.
190	6' 4"	Antique	on request
215	7' 2"	Polished Ebony	52,600.
275	9' 1"	Polished Ebony	106,000.

Gaveau

Verticals

Model	Size	Style and Finish	Price*
Etude	44"	Polished Ebony	9,215.
Etude	44"	Walnut	8,790.
Etude	44"	Polished White	9,215.
Arpège	46"	Polished Ebony	10,350.
Arpège	46"	Polished White	10,350.
Cadence	46"	Polished Ebony	10,775.
Cadence	46"	Polished White	10,775.
Florilège	47"	Polished Ebony	12,192.
Florilège	47"	Polished White	12,192.
Romantica	47"	Walnut	12,476.

George Steck — see "Steck, George"

Grotrian

Verticals

Model	Size	Style and Finish	Price*
Caret	44"	Polished Ebony	19,000.
Caret	44"	Polished Walnut	20,000.
Caret	44"	Polished Mahogany	20,000.
Classic	49"	Polished Ebony	23,800.
Classic	49"	Polished Walnut	25,400.
Classic	49"	Polished Mahogany	25,400.
Concertino	52"	Polished Ebony	27,200.

Grands

Model	Size	Style and Finish	Price*
Chambre	5' 4"	Ebony	44,600.
Chambre	5' 4"	Polished Ebony	49,000.
Chambre	5' 4"	Polished Walnut	53,800.
Cabinet	6' 3"	Ebony	49,400.
Cabinet	6' 3"	Polished Ebony	54,000.
Cabinet	6' 3"	Polished Walnut	59,000.
Concert	7' 4"	Ebony	60,800.
Concert	7' 4"	Polished Ebony	65,000.
Concert Royal	9' 2"	Polished Ebony	75,400.

*For explanation of terms and prices, please see pages 45–50.

Model	Size	Style and Finish	Price*
Haessler			
Verticals			
115 K	45"	Polished Ebony	12,118.
115 K	45"	Waxed Alder	11,880.
115 K	45"	Beech	11,880.
115 K	45"	Ash	11,880.
115 K	45"	Polished White	12,654.
118 K	46"	Polished Ebony	13,530.
118 K	46"	Ebony with Walnut Accent	14,626.
118 K	46"	Mahogany	12,796.
118 K	46"	Polished Mahogany	14,248.
118 K	46"	Walnut	12,796.
118 K	46"	Polished Walnut	14,248.
118 K	46"	Cherry	13,192.
118 K	46"	Polished Cherry	14,646.
118 K	46"	Cherry with Yew Inlay	13,988.
118 K	46"	Polished Cherry with Yew Inlay	15,440.
118 K	46"	Oak	12,796.
118 K	46"	Polished White	14,088.
118 KM	46"	Polished Ebony	14,328.
118 KM	46"	Polished White	14,924.
118 CH	46"	Mahogany	13,850.
118 CH	46"	Polished Mahogany	15,440.
118 CH	46"	Walnut	14,188.
118 CH	46"	Polished Walnut	15,780.
124 K	49"	Polished Ebony	14,486.
124 K	49"	Ebony with Walnut Accent	15,302.
124 K	49"	Mahogany	14,088.
124 K	49"	Polished Mahogany	15,680.
124 K	49"	Walnut	14,088.
124 K	49"	Polished Walnut	15,680.
124 K	49"	Cherry	14,546.
124 K	49"	Polished Cherry	16,136.
124 K	49"	Cherry with Yew Inlay	15,342.
124 K	49"	Polished Cherry with Yew Inlay	16,934.
124 K	49"	Polished White	15,082.
124 KM	49"	Polished Ebony	15,042.
124 KM	49"	Polished White	15,042.
132	52"	Polished Ebony	20,220.

Model	Size	Style and Finish	Price*
Grands			
175	5' 8"	Ebony	37,722.
175	5' 8"	Polished Ebony	38,494.
175	5' 8"	Mahogany	37,236.
175	5' 8"	Polished Mahogany	40,024.
175	5' 8"	Polished Pyramid Mahogany	49,980.
175	5' 8"	Walnut	38,952.
175	5' 8"	Polished Walnut	42,322.
175	5' 8"	Open-Pore Walnut	37,016.
175	5' 8"	Cherry	37,236.
175	5' 8"	Polished Cherry	40,024.
175	5' 8"	Polished Bubinga	40,024.
175	5' 8"	Polished White	40,420.
175	5' 8"	French Baroque Dark Walnut	51,896.
175	5' 8"	French Baroque White	62,234.
175	5' 8"	Classic Victorian Polished Ebony	44,236.
175	5' 8"	Classic Victorian Polished Mahogany	45,998.
175	5' 8"	Classic Alexandra Polished Ebony	44,236.
175	5' 8"	Classic Alexandra Polished Mahogany	45,998.
186	6' 1"	Ebony	39,264.
186	6' 1"	Polished Ebony	41,850.
186	6' 1"	Mahogany	39,970.
186	6' 1"	Polished Mahogany	42,964.
186	6' 1"	Polished Pyramid Mahogany	53,656.
186	6' 1"	Walnut	41,814.
186	6' 1"	Polished Walnut	45,432.
186	6' 1"	Open-Pore Walnut	39,732.
186	6' 1"	Cherry	39,970.
186	6' 1"	Polished Cherry	42,964.
186	6' 1"	Polished Bubinga	42,964.
186	6' 1"	Polished White	43,510.
186	6' 1"	French Baroque Dark Walnut	55,712.
186	6' 1"	French Baroque White	66,814.
186	6' 1"	Classic Victorian Polished Ebony	47,488.
186	6' 1"	Classic Victorian Polished Mahogany	49,380.
186	6' 1"	Classic Alexandra Polished Ebony	47,488.
186	6' 1"	Classic Alexandra Polished Mahogany	49,380.

*For explanation of terms and prices, please see pages 45–50.

Hallet, Davis & Co. — see "Maeari / Hallet, Davis & Co."

Hoffmann, W.

Verticals

Model	Size	Style and Finish	Price
H-115	45-1/2"	Polished Ebony	14,320.
H-115	45-1/2"	Oak	14,160.
H-115	45-1/2"	Mahogany	14,160.
H-115	45-1/2"	Polished Mahogany	15,500.
H-115	45-1/2"	Walnut	14,160.
H-115	45-1/2"	Polished Walnut	15,500.
H-115	45-1/2"	Cherry	14,160.
H-115	45-1/2"	Polished Cherry	15,500.
H-115	45-1/2"	Polished White	15,300.
H-117	46"	Polished Ebony	10,600.
H-120	47"	Polished Ebony	15,480.
H-120	47"	Oak	15,140.
H-120	47"	Mahogany	15,140.
H-120	47"	Polished Mahogany	16,720.
H-120	47"	Walnut	15,140.
H-120	47"	Polished Walnut	16,720.
H-120	47"	Cherry	15,140.
H-120	47"	Polished Cherry	16,720.
H-120	47"	Polished White	16,160.
H-120	47"	Polished Blue	16,720.
H-124	49"	Polished Ebony	16,580.
H-124	49"	Oak	16,440.
H-124	49"	Mahogany	16,440.
H-124	49"	Polished Mahogany	17,840.
H-124	49"	Walnut	16,440.
H-124	49"	Polished Walnut	17,840.
H-124	49"	Cherry	16,440.
H-124	49"	Polished Cherry	17,840.
H-124	49"	Polished White	17,300.

Grands

Model	Size	Style and Finish	Price
H-173	5' 7"	Polished Ebony	28,540.
H-173	5' 7"	Polished Mahogany	29,940.
H-190	6' 3"	Polished Ebony	32,760.

Model	Size	Style and Finish	Price*

Hyundai

Verticals

Model	Size	Style and Finish	Price*
U-800	42"	Continental Polished Ebony	3,998.
U-800	42"	Continental Walnut	3,758.
U-800	42"	Continental Polished Walnut	4,300.
U-800	42"	Continental Polished Mahogany	4,300.
U-800	42"	Continental Polished Ivory	3,998.
U-824F	43"	French Walnut	4,998.
U-824F	43"	French Brown Oak	4,998.
U-824F	43"	French Cherry	4,998.
U-824M	43"	Mediterranean Brown Oak	4,998.
U-824M	43"	Mediterranean Walnut	4,998.
U-822	45"	Continental Polished Ebony	4,698.
U-822	45"	Continental Polished Mahogany	4,998.
U-852	46"	Ebony	5,598.
U-852	46"	Polished Ebony	5,598.
U-852	46"	Brown Oak	5,598.
U-852	46"	Walnut	5,198.
U-842	46"	Chippendale Polished Mahogany	5,598.
U-832	48"	Ebony	5,198.
U-832	48"	Polished Ebony	5,198.
U-832	48"	Walnut	5,398.
U-832	48"	Polished Walnut	5,398.
U-832	48"	Brown Oak	5,398.
U-832	48"	Polished Brown Oak	5,398.
U-832	48"	Polished Mahogany	5,398.
U-837	52"	Ebony	5,598.
U-837	52"	Polished Ebony	5,698.
U-837	52"	Walnut	5,598.
U-837	52"	Polished Walnut	5,798.
U-837	52"	Polished Mahogany	5,798.

Grands

Model	Size	Style and Finish	Price*
G-50A	4' 7"	Ebony	9,898.
G-50A	4' 7"	Polished Ebony	9,998.
G-50A	4' 7"	Walnut	10,398.
G-50A	4' 7"	Polished Walnut	10,398.

*For explanation of terms and prices, please see pages 45–50.

Model	Size	Style and Finish	Price*
Hyundai (continued)			
G-50A	4' 7"	Polished Mahogany	10,398.
G-50A	4' 7"	Brown Oak	10,398.
G-50A	4' 7"	Polished Brown Oak	10,398.
G-50A	4' 7"	Polished Natural Oak	10,398.
G-50A	4' 7"	Cherry	10,398.
G-50A	4' 7"	Polished Ivory	10,198.
G-50A	4' 7"	Polished White	10,198.
G-50AF	4' 7"	Queen Anne Walnut	11,900.
G-50AF	4' 7"	Queen Anne Polished Walnut	11,900.
G-50AF	4' 7"	Queen Anne Brown Oak	11,900.
G-50AF	4' 7"	Queen Anne Polished Brown Oak	11,900.
G-50AF	4' 7"	Queen Anne Polished Mahogany	11,900.
G-50AF	4' 7"	Queen Anne Cherry	11,900.
G-50AF	4' 7"	Queen Anne Polished Ivory	11,900.
G-50AF	4' 7"	Queen Anne Polished White	11,900.
G-80A	5' 1"	Ebony	11,398.
G-80A	5' 1"	Polished Ebony	11,498.
G-80A	5' 1"	Walnut	11,898.
G-80A	5' 1"	Polished Walnut	11,898.
G-80A	5' 1"	Polished Natural Oak	11,898.
G-80A	5' 1"	Brown Oak	11,898.
G-80A	5' 1"	Polished Mahogany	11,898.
G-80A	5' 1"	Cherry	11,898.
G-80A	5' 1"	Polished Ivory	11,698.
G-80A	5' 1"	Polished White	11,698.
G-80AF	5' 1"	Queen Anne Polished Mahogany	14,098.
G-80B	5' 1"	Chippendale Polished Mahogany	14,098.
G-81	5' 9"	Chippendale Polished Mahogany	15,398.
G-82	5' 9"	Ebony	12,798.
G-82	5' 9"	Polished Ebony	12,898.
G-82	5' 9"	Walnut	13,298.
G-82	5' 9"	Polished Walnut	13,298.
G-82	5' 9"	Polished Natural Oak	13,298.
G-82	5' 9"	Brown Oak	13,298.
G-82	5' 9"	Polished Brown Oak	13,298.
G-82	5' 9"	Polished Mahogany	13,298.

Model	Size	Style and Finish	Price*
G-82	5' 9"	Cherry	13,298.
G-82	5' 9"	Polished Ivory	13,098.
G-82	5' 9"	Polished White	13,098.
G-82AF	5' 9"	Queen Anne Polished Mahogany	15,398.
G-84	6' 1"	Ebony	13,498.
G-84	6' 1"	Polished Ebony	13,598.
G-84	6' 1"	Walnut	13,998.
G-84	6' 1"	Polished Walnut	13,998.
G-84	6' 1"	Brown Oak	13,998.
G-84	6' 1"	Polished Mahogany	13,998.
G-84	6' 1"	Polished Ivory	13,798.
G-84	6' 1"	Polished White	13,798.
G-85	6' 10"	Ebony	17,398.
G-85	6' 10"	Polished Ebony	17,398.

Kawai

Verticals

Model	Size	Style and Finish	Price*
504-M	43"	Mediterranean Oak	4,090.
504-T	43"	Mahogany	4,090.
504-F	43"	French Provincial Cherry	4,190.
504-Q	43"	Queen Anne Mahogany	4,190.
505-M	43"	Mediterranean Oak	4,530.
505-T	43"	Mahogany	4,530.
505-F	43"	French Provincial Cherry	4,650.
505-Q	43"	Queen Anne Mahogany	4,650.
605-M	44"	Mediterranean Oak	5,350.
605-T	44"	Mahogany	5,410.
605-CF	44"	Country French Oak	5,450.
605-F	44"	French Provincial Cherry	5,450.
CX-5H	45"	Ebony	3,990.
CX-5H	45"	Polished Ebony	3,990.
CX-5H	45"	Oak	4,290.
CX-5H	45"	Mahogany	4,790.
CX-5H	45"	Polished Mahogany	4,990.
AT-105	45"	CX-5H Polished Ebony with AnyTime	5,990.
902-M	46"	Mediterranean Oak	6,070.
902-F	46"	French Provincial Cherry	6,290.

*For explanation of terms and prices, please see pages 45–50.

Model	Size	Style and Finish	Price*
Kawai (continued)			
902-T	46"	Mahogany	6,290.
UST-7	46"	Ebony	6,180.
UST-7	46"	Oak	6,330.
UST-7	46"	Walnut	6,370.
UST-8C	46"	Ebony	5,190.
UST-8C	46"	Walnut	5,190.
UST-8C	46"	Oak	5,190.
CX-21	48"	Polished Ebony	5,590.
CX-21	48"	Mahogany	5,890.
CX-21	48"	Polished Snow White	5,590.
NS-20A	49"	Polished Ebony	7,210.
NS-20A	49"	Oak	7,630.
NS-20A	49"	Walnut	7,850.
NS-20A	49"	Polished Walnut	8,330.
NS-20A	49"	Polished Sapeli Mahogany	8,190.
US-6X	52"	Polished Ebony	9,590.
US-6X	52"	Polished Walnut	10,850.
US-8X	52"	Polished Ebony	11,750.
Grands			
GM-2A	5'	Ebony	11,090.
GM-2A	5'	Polished Ebony	11,190.
GM-2A	5'	Polished Snow White	11,990.
GE-1A	5' 1"	Ebony	13,190.
GE-1A	5' 1"	Polished Ebony	13,390.
GE-1A	5' 1"	Walnut	14,990.
GE-1A	5' 1"	Mahogany	15,390.
GE-1A	5' 1"	Sapeli Mahogany	15,390.
GE-1A	5' 1"	Polished Snow White	14,590.
GE-1AS	5' 1"	Polished Ebony	13,590.
RX-1	5' 5"	Ebony	16,690.
RX-1	5' 5"	Polished Ebony	16,990.
RX-1	5' 5"	Walnut	18,990.
RX-1	5' 5"	Polished Walnut	19,790.
RX-1	5' 5"	Polished Sapeli Mahogany	19,590.
RX-1	5' 5"	Polished Snow White	18,790.

Model	Size	Style and Finish	Price*
GE-3	5' 9"	Polished Ebony	16,790.
GE-3	5' 9"	Polished Snow White	18,790.
RX-2	5' 10"	Ebony	18,790.
RX-2	5' 10"	Polished Ebony	19,190.
RX-2	5' 10"	Walnut	20,790.
RX-2	5' 10"	Polished Walnut	21,590.
RX-2	5' 10"	Oak	19,790.
RX-2	5' 10"	Polished Mahogany	21,790.
RX-2	5' 10"	Polished Sapeli Mahogany	21,190.
RX-2	5' 10"	Polished Rosewood	25,090.
RX-2	5' 10"	Polished Snow White	20,390.
RX-2F	5' 10"	French Provincial Polished Mahogany	25,090.
RX-3	6' 1"	Ebony	25,290.
RX-3	6' 1"	Polished Ebony	26,190.
RX-3	6' 1"	Walnut	28,990.
RX-3	6' 1"	Polished Snow White	26,990.
RX-A	6' 5"	Polished Ebony	51,990.
RX-5	6' 6"	Ebony	27,990.
RX-5	6' 6"	Polished Ebony	28,390.
RX-6	7'	Ebony	30,990.
RX-6	7'	Polished Ebony	31,390.
RX-7	7' 6"	Ebony	35,790.
RX-7	7' 6"	Polished Ebony	35,990.
GS-100	9' 1"	Ebony	66,790.
GS-100	9' 1"	Polished Ebony	68,790.
EX	9' 1"	Polished Ebony	98,990.
EX-G	9' 1"	Polished Ebony	108,990.

Kemble

Verticals

Cambridge 10	43"	Continental Polished Ebony	6,820.
Cambridge 10	43"	Continental Mahogany	6,160.
Cambridge 10	43"	Continental Polished Mahogany	6,820.
Cambridge 10	43"	Continental Walnut	6,160.
Oxford	43"	Polished Ebony	7,040.
Oxford	43"	Mahogany	6,380.
Oxford	43"	Polished Mahogany	7,040.

*For explanation of terms and prices, please see pages 45–50.

Model	Size	Style and Finish	Price*

Kemble (continued)

Oxford	43"	Walnut	6,380.
Oxford	43"	Polished Walnut	7,040.
Oxford	43"	Beech	7,040.
Cambridge 15	45"	Continental Mahogany	6,820.
Cambridge 15	45"	Continental Polished Mahogany	7,480.
Cambridge 15	45"	Continental Cherry	7,040.
Traditional	45"	Polished Ebony	7,700.
Traditional	45"	Polished Mahogany	7,700.
Traditional	45"	Alder	7,700.
Prestige	45"	Cherry with Yew Inlay	8,700.
Empire	45"	Empire Polished Mahogany	8,920.
K121Z	48"	Polished Ebony	8,900.
K121Z	48"	Polished Mahogany	8,900.
K121Z	48"	Polished Walnut	8,900.
K121Z	48"	Polished Ebony w/Burr Walnut Panel	9,400.

Silent Verticals

KS-15	45"	Continental Walnut	8,700.
KS Trad.	45"	Polished Ebony	9,360.
KS Empire	45"	Empire Polished Mahogany	10,780.

Kingsburg

Verticals

109A	43"	Continental Polished Ebony	2,790.
109A	43"	Continental Polished Mahogany	2,870.
109A	43"	Continental Polished Walnut	2,870.
109B	43"	Polished Ebony	2,870.
109B	43"	Polished Mahogany	2,950.
109B	43"	Polished Walnut	2,950.
109C	43"	Polished Ebony	2,870.
109C	43"	Polished Mahogany	2,950.
109C	43"	Polished Walnut	2,950.
F-113	44"	French Provincial Mahogany	3,500.
S-115	45"	Polished Ebony	3,140.
S-115	45"	Polished Mahogany	3,200.
S-115	45"	Polished Walnut	3,200.

Model	Size	Style and Finish	Price*
LM-116	46"	French Provincial Mahogany	3,440.
LM-117	46-1/2"	Walnut	3,780.
122-SL	48"	Polished Ebony	3,700.
122-SL	48"	Polished Mahogany	4,000.
122-SL	48"	Polished Walnut	4,000.
Grands			
G-158	5' 2"	Polished Ebony	10,380.
G-185	6' 1"	Polished Ebony	11,780.

Knabe, (Wm.)

The prices below include a factory-installed PianoDisc PDS 128 Plus playback system. Subtract $110 for a PianoCD system. Add $1,299 each for a SymphonyPro Sound Module or a TFT MIDI Record System. Subtract $1,800 for a factory-installed GT-360 QuietTime system instead of the PDS 128 Plus. Subtract $4,000 for a regular acoustic piano without any extra equipment.

Verticals

KB-420	42"	Continental Polished Ebony	7,190.
KB-420	42"	Continental Polished Mahogany	7,290.
KN-420	42"	Continental Ebony	9,204.
KN-420	42"	Continental Polished Ebony	9,204.
KN-420	42"	Continental Walnut	9,284.
KN-420	42"	Continental Polished Walnut	9,284.
KN-420	42"	Continental Polished Mahogany	9,284.
KN-420	42"	Continental Polished Ivory	9,204.
KN-420	42"	Continental Polished White	9,204.
KB-43	43"	French Provincial Oak	7,490.
KB-43	43"	French Provincial Cherry	7,490.
KN-43	43"	Queen Anne Oak	10,032.
KN-43	43"	Queen Anne Cherry	10,032.
KN-460	46"	Ebony	9,390.
KN-460	46"	Oak	9,590.
KB-480	48"	Polished Ebony	7,790.
KB-480	48"	Polished Mahogany	7,890.
KN-480	48"	Ebony	10,872.
KN-480	48"	Polished Ebony	10,872.
KN-480	48"	Walnut	11,166.

*For explanation of terms and prices, please see pages 45–50.

Model	Size	Style and Finish	Price*
Knabe (continued)			
KN-480	48"	Polished Walnut	11,166.
KN-480	48"	Polished Mahogany	11,166.
KN-480	48"	Polished Ivory	10,872.
KN-480	48"	Polished White	10,872.
KN-480NFI	48"	Open-Pore Walnut	11,254.
Grands			
KN-500	4' 11"	Ebony	17,586.
KN-500	4' 11"	Polished Ebony	17,586.
KN-500	4' 11"	Walnut	18,366.
KN-500	4' 11"	Polished Walnut	18,366.
KN-500	4' 11"	Mahogany	18,366.
KN-500	4' 11"	Polished Mahogany	18,366.
KN-500	4' 11"	Golden Oak	18,366.
KN-500	4' 11"	Bubinga	18,366.
KN-500	4' 11"	Polished Ivory	17,586.
KN-500	4' 11"	Polished White	17,586.
KN-500	4' 11"	Queen Anne Mahogany	20,128.
KN-500	4' 11"	Queen Anne Polished Mahogany	20,128.
KN-500	4' 11"	Queen Anne Cherry	20,128.
KN-500	4' 11"	Queen Anne Golden Oak	20,128.
KN-520	5' 2"	Ebony	18,698.
KN-520	5' 2"	Polished Ebony	18,698.
KN-520	5' 2"	Walnut	19,264.
KN-520	5' 2"	Polished Walnut	19,264.
KN-520	5' 2"	Mahogany	19,264.
KN-520	5' 2"	Polished Mahogany	19,264.
KN-520	5' 2"	Golden Oak	19,264.
KN-520	5' 2"	Bubinga	19,264.
KN-520	5' 2"	Polished Ivory	18,698.
KN-520	5' 2"	Polished White	18,698.
KN-520	5' 2"	Queen Anne Cherry	22,532.
KN-520	5' 2"	Queen Anne Mahogany	22,532.
KN-520	5' 2"	Queen Anne Golden Oak	22,532.
KN-590	5' 9"	Ebony	20,740.
KN-590	5' 9"	Polished Ebony	20,740.

Model	Size	Style and Finish	Price*
KN-590	5' 9"	Walnut	21,420.
KN-590	5' 9"	Polished Walnut	21,420.
KN-590	5' 9"	Polished Mahogany	21,420.
KN-590	5' 9"	Polished Ivory	20,740.
KN-590	5' 9"	Polished White	20,740.
KN-590	5' 9"	Empire Inlay Polished Mahogany	24,460.
KN-610	6' 1"	Ebony	21,192.
KN-610	6' 1"	Polished Ebony	21,192.
KN-610	6' 1"	Walnut	22,996.
KN-610	6' 1"	Polished Walnut	22,996.
KN-610	6' 1"	Polished Mahogany	22,996.
KN-610	6' 1"	Polished Ivory	21,192.
KN-610	6' 1"	Polished White	21,192.
KN-700	6' 10"	Ebony	27,120.
KN-700	6' 10"	Polished Ebony	27,120.

Knight, Alfred

Prices are FOB England and do not include duty, freight, and other costs of importing. Oak, ash, and cherry are available at the same price as mahogany. Polished white is available at the same price as polished ebony.

Verticals

Model	Size	Style and Finish	Price
York	44"	Polished Ebony	10,320.
York	44"	Mahogany	9,200.
York	44"	Polished Mahogany	10,320.
York	44"	Walnut	9,200.
York	44"	Polished Walnut	10,320.
York	44"	Teak	9,200.
London	44"	Polished Ebony	11,280.
London	44"	Mahogany	10,040.
London	44"	Polished Mahogany	11,280.
London	44"	Walnut	10,040.
London	44"	Polished Walnut	11,280.
K10 Slimline	44"	Polished Ebony	11,360.
K10 Slimline	44"	Mahogany	10,260.
K10 Slimline	44"	Polished Mahogany	11,360.
K10 Slimline	44"	Walnut	10,260.
K10 Slimline	44"	Polished Walnut	11,360.

*For explanation of terms and prices, please see pages 45–50.

Model	Size	Style and Finish	Price*

Knight, Alfred (continued)

Model	Size	Style and Finish	Price*
K10 Slimline	44"	Teak	10,260.
K10 School	44"	Mahogany	10,800.
K10 School	44"	Oak	10,800.
Savoy	48"	Polished Ebony	13,780.
Savoy	48"	Mahogany	12,360.
Savoy	48"	Polished Mahogany	13,780.
Savoy	48"	Walnut	12,360.
Savoy	48"	Polished Walnut	13,780.

Kohler & Campbell

Verticals

Model	Size	Style and Finish	Price*
SKV-108S	42"	Continental Ebony	3,590.
SKV-108S	42"	Continental Polished Ebony	3,590.
SKV-108S	42"	Continental Walnut	3,790.
SKV-108S	42"	Continental Polished Walnut	3,790.
SKV-108S	42"	Continental Polished Mahogany	3,790.
SKV-108S	42"	Continental Oak	3,790.
SKV-108S	42"	Continental Polished Oak	3,790.
SKV-108S	42"	Continental Polished Ivory	3,590.
SKV-108S	42"	Continental Polished White	3,590.
KC 108	43"	Continental Polished Ebony	2,990.
KC 108	43"	Continental Walnut	2,790.
KC 108	43"	Continental Polished Walnut	3,090.
KC 108	43"	Continental Polished Mahogany	3,090.
KC 108	43"	Continental Polished Ivory	3,090.
KC 108	43"	Continental Polished White	3,090.
KC 043M	43"	Mediterranean Brown Oak	3,290.
KC 043F	43"	French Provincial Brown Oak	3,390.
KC 043F	43"	French Provincial Cherry	3,390.
KC 112	44"	Polished Ebony	3,190.
KC 112	44"	Walnut	2,990.
KC 112	44"	Polished Walnut	3,290.
KC 112	44"	Polished Mahogany	3,290.
KC 112	44"	Polished Ivory	3,290.
KC 112	44"	Polished White	3,290.

Model	Size	Style and Finish	Price*
SKV-465S	46-1/2"	Ebony	4,390.
SKV-465S	46-1/2"	Polished Ebony	4,390.
SKV-465S	46-1/2"	Walnut	4,590.
SKV-465S	46-1/2"	Polished Walnut	4,590.
SKV-465S	46-1/2"	Mahogany	4,590.
SKV-465S	46-1/2"	Polished Mahogany	4,590.
SKV-465S	46-1/2"	Oak	4,590.
SKV-465S	46-1/2"	Polished Oak	4,590.
SKV-118FA	46-1/2"	French Polished Mahogany	5,190.
SKV-118FA	46-1/2"	French Polished Walnut	5,190.
KC 118M	46-1/2"	Mediterranean Brown Oak	3,790.
KC 118F	46-1/2"	French Brown Oak	3,990.
KC 118F	46-1/2"	French Provincial Cherry	3,990.
KC 118T	46-1/2"	Mahogany	3,990.
KC 118T	46-1/2"	Cherry	3,990.
SKV-48S	48"	Ebony	4,590.
SKV-48S	48"	Polished Ebony	4,590.
SKV-48S	48"	Walnut	4,790.
SKV-48S	48"	Polished Walnut	4,790.
SKV-48S	48"	Polished Mahogany	4,790.
SKV-48S	48"	Oak	4,790.
SKV-48S	48"	Polished Oak	4,790.
SKV-48S	48"	Polished Ivory	4,590.
SKV-48S	48"	Polished White	4,590.
KC 121F	48"	Polished Ebony	3,990.
KC 121F	48"	Polished Mahogany	4,390.
MKV-48LD	48"	Ebony	5,190.
MKV-48LD	48"	Polished Ebony	5,190.
MKV-48LD	48"	Walnut	5,390.
MKV-48LD	48"	Polished Walnut	5,390.
MKV-48LD	48"	Mahogany	5,390.
MKV-48LD	48"	Polished Mahogany	5,390.
SKV-52S	52"	Ebony	5,390.
SKV-52S	52"	Polished Ebony	5,390.
SKV-52S	52"	Walnut	5,590.
SKV-52S	52"	Polished Walnut	5,590.
SKV-52S	52"	Polished Mahogany	5,590.

*For explanation of terms and prices, please see pages 45–50.

Model	Size	Style and Finish	Price*

Kohler & Campbell (continued)

Model	Size	Style and Finish	Price*
SKV-52S	52"	Polished White	5,390.
MKV-52GD	52"	Ebony	5,990.
MKV-52GD	52"	Polished Ebony	5,990.
MKV-52GD	52"	Mahogany	6,390.
MKV-52GD	52"	Polished Mahogany	6,390.

Grands

Model	Size	Style and Finish	Price*
KIG 47	4' 7"	Polished Ebony	7,190.
KIG 47	4' 7"	Polished White	7,190.
KIG 47	4' 7"	Polished Ivory	7,190.
SKG-400S	4' 7"	Ebony	8,790.
SKG-400S	4' 7"	Polished Ebony	8,790.
SKG-400S	4' 7"	Walnut	9,190.
SKG-400S	4' 7"	Polished Walnut	9,190.
SKG-400S	4' 7"	Mahogany	9,190.
SKG-400S	4' 7"	Polished Mahogany	9,190.
SKG-400S	4' 7"	Oak	9,190.
SKG-400S	4' 7"	Polished Oak	9,190.
SKG-400S	4' 7"	Cherry	9,190.
SKG-400S	4' 7"	Polished Ivory	8,990.
SKG-400S	4' 7"	Polished White	8,990.
SKG-400SKAF	4' 7"	French Provincial—all finishes (satin)	10,890.
SKG-400SKBF	4' 7"	French Provincial—all finishes (polish)	11,290.
SKG-500S	5' 1"	Ebony	9,990.
SKG-500S	5' 1"	Polished Ebony	9,990.
SKG-500S	5' 1"	Walnut	10,390.
SKG-500S	5' 1"	Polished Walnut	10,390.
SKG-500S	5' 1'	Mahogany	10,390.
SKG-500S	5' 1"	Polished Mahogany	10,390.
SKG-500S	5' 1"	Oak	10,390.
SKG-500S	5' 1"	Polished Oak	10,390.
SKG-500S	5' 1"	Cherry	10,390.
SKG-500S	5' 1"	Polished Ivory	10,190.
SKG-500S	5' 1"	Polished White	10,190.
SKG-500SKAF	5' 1"	French Provincial—all finishes (polish)	11,590.
SKG-500SKBF	5' 1"	French Provincial—all finishes (polish)	11,990.

Model	Size	Style and Finish	Price*
SKG-600S	5' 9"	Ebony	11,190.
SKG-600S	5' 9"	Polished Ebony	11,190.
SKG-600S	5' 9"	Walnut	11,590.
SKG-600S	5' 9"	Polished Walnut	11,590.
SKG-600S	5' 9"	Mahogany	11,590.
SKG-600S	5' 9"	Polished Mahogany	11,590.
SKG-600S	5' 9"	Oak	11,590.
SKG-600S	5' 9"	Polished Oak	11,590.
SKG-600S	5' 9"	Cherry	11,590.
SKG-600S	5' 9"	Polished Ivory	11,390.
SKG-600S	5' 9"	White	11,190.
SKG-600S	5' 9"	Polished White	11,190.
SKG-600SL	5' 9"	Empire Ebony	12,190.
SKG-600SL	5' 9"	Empire Polished Ebony	12,190.
SKG-600SL	5' 9"	Empire Mahogany	12,590.
SKG-600SL	5' 9"	Empire Polished Mahogany	12,590.
SKG-650S	6' 1"	Ebony	11,990.
SKG-650S	6' 1"	Polished Ebony	11,990.
SKG-650S	6' 1"	Walnut	12,590.
SKG-650S	6' 1"	Polished Walnut	12,590.
SKG-650S	6' 1"	Mahogany	12,590.
SKG-650S	6' 1"	Polished Mahogany	12,590.
SKG-650S	6' 1"	Oak	12,590.
SKG-650S	6' 1"	Polished Oak	12,590.
SKG-650S	6' 1"	Cherry	12,590.
SKG-650SL	6' 1"	Empire Ebony	12,990.
SKG-650SL	6' 1"	Empire Polished Ebony	12,990.
SKG-650SL	6' 1"	Empire Mahogany	13,590.
SKG-650SL	6' 1"	Empire Polished Mahogany	13,590.
KFM-650S	6' 1"	Ebony	17,500.
KFM-650S	6' 1"	Polished Ebony	17,500.
KFM-650S	6' 1"	All other finishes (see SKG-650S)	17,900.
KFM-650SL	6' 1"	Empire Ebony	18,500.
KFM-650SL	6' 1"	Empire Polished Ebony	18,500.
KFM-650SL	6' 1"	Empire Mahogany	18,900.
KFM-650SL	6' 1"	Empire Polished Mahogany	18,900.
KFM-700S	6' 8"	Ebony	19,990.

*For explanation of terms and prices, please see pages 45–50.

Kohler & Campbell (continued)

Model	Size	Style and Finish	Price
KFM-700S	6' 8"	Polished Ebony	19,990.
KFM-700S	6' 8"	All other finishes (see SKG-650S)	20,390.
KFM-800S	7'	Ebony	21,990.
KFM-800S	7'	Polished Ebony	21,990.
KFM-900S	9' 1"	Ebony	45,990.
KFM-900S	9' 1"	Polished Ebony	45,990.
KFM-900S	9' 1"	All other finishes (see SKG-650S)	47,990.

Krakauer

Verticals

Model	Size	Style and Finish	Price
K433	43"	French Cherry	2,890.
K434	43"	French Oak	2,890.
K435	43"	Oak	2,890.
K436	43"	Cherry	2,890.
K110 B	43"	Polished Ebony	2,890.
K110 R	43"	Polished Mahogany	2,890.
K110 T	43"	Polished Walnut	2,890.
K110 W	43"	Polished White	2,890.
K120 B	48"	Polished Ebony	3,190.
K120 R	48"	Polished Mahogany	3,190.
K120 T	48"	Polished Walnut	3,190.
K120 W	48"	Polished White	3,190.
K132 B	52"	Polished Ebony	3,610.
K132 R	52"	Polished Mahogany	3,610.
K132 T	52"	Polished Walnut	3,610.
K132 W	52"	Polished White	3,610.

Maeari / Hallet, Davis & Co.

The models listed below are for Maeari pianos. For Hallet, Davis & Co. vertical models, substitute HU for MU in the model number; for Hallet, Davis grands, substitute HG for G. Most of the models below are available in either name; styles and finishes available only as Maeari are marked *.

Verticals

Model	Size	Style and Finish	Price
MU-800	42"	Continental Polished Ebony	3,998.
MU-800	42"	Continental Walnut	3,758.

Model	Size	Style and Finish	Price*
MU-800	42"	Continental Polished Walnut*	4,300.
MU-800	42"	Continental Polished Mahogany	4,300.
MU-800	42"	Continental Polished White	3,998.
MU-800	42"	Continental Polished Ivory	3,998.
MU-824F	43"	French Walnut	4,998.
MU-824F	43"	French Brown Oak	4,998.
MU-824F	43"	French Cherry	4,998.
MU-824M	43"	Mediterranean Walnut	4,998.
MU-824M	43"	Mediterranean Brown Oak	4,998.
MU-824M	43"	Mediterranean Cherry	4,998.
MU-842	46"	Chippendale Polished Mahogany	5,598.
MU-852	46"	Ebony	5,598.
MU-852	46"	Polished Ebony	5,598.
MU-852	46"	Brown Oak	5,598.
MU-832	48"	Ebony	5,198.
MU-832	48"	Polished Ebony	5,198.
MU-832	48"	Walnut	4,998.
MU-832	48"	Polished Walnut	5,398.
MU-832	48"	Polished Mahogany	5,398.
MU-837	52"	Polished Ebony	5,698.
MU-837	52"	Walnut	5,598.
MU-837	52"	Polished Walnut	5,798.
MU-837	52"	Polished Mahogany	5,798.
Grands			
G-450A	4' 7"	Ebony	9,898.
G-450A	4' 7"	Polished Ebony	9,998.
G-450A	4' 7"	Walnut	10,398.
G-450A	4' 7"	Polished Walnut	10,398.
G-450A	4' 7"	Polished Mahogany	10,398.
G-450A	4' 7"	Cherry	10,398.
G-450A	4' 7"	Polished Natural Oak*	10,398.
G-450A	4' 7"	Brown Oak	10,398.
G-450A	4' 7"	Polished Brown Oak*	10,398.
G-450A	4' 7"	Polished Ivory	10,198.
G-450A	4' 7"	Polished White	10,198.
G-450AF	4' 7"	Queen Anne Polished Ebony*	11,900.
G-450AF	4' 7"	Queen Anne Walnut*	11,900.

*For explanation of terms and prices, please see pages 45–50.

Model	Size	Style and Finish	Price*

Maeari / Hallet, Davis & Co. (continued)

Model	Size	Style and Finish	Price*
G-450AF	4' 7"	Queen Anne Polished Walnut*	11,900.
G-450AF	4' 7"	Queen Anne Polished Mahogany	11,900.
G-450AF	4' 7"	Queen Anne Cherry	11,900.
G-450AF	4' 7"	Queen Anne Brown Oak*	11,900.
G-450AF	4' 7"	Queen Anne Polished Brown Oak*	11,900.
G-450AF	4' 7"	Queen Anne Polished Ivory*	11,900.
G-450AF	4' 7"	Queen Anne Polished White*	11,900.
G-480A	5' 1"	Ebony	11,398.
G-480A	5' 1"	Polished Ebony	11,498.
G-480A	5' 1"	Walnut	11,898.
G-480A	5' 1"	Polished Walnut	11,898.
G-480A	5' 1"	Polished Mahogany	11,898.
G-480A	5' 1"	Cherry	11,898.
G-480A	5' 1"	Polished Natural Oak*	11,898.
G-480A	5' 1"	Brown Oak*	11,898.
G-480A	5' 1"	Polished Ivory	11,698.
G-480A	5' 1"	Polished White	11,698.
G-480B	5' 1"	Chippendale Polished Mahogany	14,098.
G-480AF	5' 1"	Queen Anne Polished Mahogany	14,098.
G-481	5' 9"	Chippendale Polished Mahogany	15,398.
G-482	5' 9"	Ebony	12,798.
G-482	5' 9"	Polished Ebony	12,898.
G-482	5' 9"	Walnut	13,298.
G-482	5' 9"	Polished Walnut	13,298.
G-482	5' 9"	Polished Mahogany	13,298.
G-482	5' 9"	Cherry*	13,298.
G-482	5' 9"	Polished Ivory*	13,098.
G-482	5' 9"	Polished White*	13,098.
G-482AF	5' 9"	Queen Anne Polished Mahogany	15,398.
G-484	6' 1"	Ebony	13,498.
G-484	6' 1"	Polished Ebony	13,598.
G-484	6' 1"	Walnut*	13,998.
G-484	6' 1"	Polished Walnut*	13,998.
G-484	6' 1"	Polished Mahogany	13,998.
G-484	6' 1"	Oak*	13,998.
G-484	6' 1"	Polished Ivory*	13,798.

Model	Size	Style and Finish	Price*
G-484	6' 1"	Polished White*	13,798.
G-485	6' 10"	Ebony	17,398.
G-485	6' 10"	Polished Ebony	17,398.

Mason & Hamlin

Verticals

50	50"	Ebony	14,192.
50	50"	Oak	14,404.
50	50"	*Mahogany*	14,404.
50	50"	*Walnut*	14,404.

Grands

A	5' 8"	Ebony	39,208.
A	5' 8"	Polished Ebony	40,268.
A	5' 8"	*Mahogany*	40,268.
A	5' 8"	*Polished Mahogany*	41,116.
A	5' 8"	*Walnut*	41,964.
A	5' 8"	*Polished Walnut*	42,812.
A	5' 8"	"Monticello" Mahogany	46,098.
BB	7'	Ebony	49,808.
BB	7'	Polished Ebony	50,868.
BB	7'	*Mahogany*	50,868.
BB	7'	*Polished Mahogany*	51,504.
BB	7'	*Walnut*	54,260.
BB	7'	*Polished Walnut*	55,108.
BB	7'	"Monticello" Mahogany	58,232.

Mecklenburg

Verticals

MS-1 OBH	48"	Polished Ebony	6,998.

Niemeyer

Verticals

NI112	44"	Continental Polished Ebony	2,700.
NI112	44"	Continental Polished Mahogany	2,700.
NI112	44"	Continental Polished Walnut	2,700.
NI112	44"	Continental Polished White	2,790.

*For explanation of terms and prices, please see pages 45–50.

Model	Size	Style and Finish	Price*

Niemeyer (continued)

Model	Size	Style and Finish	Price*
NI114	45"	Polished Ebony	2,900.
NI114	45"	Polished Mahogany	2,900.
NI115	45"	Chippendale Polished Mahogany	3,100.
NI121	48"	Polished Ebony	3,100.
NI121	48"	Polished Mahogany	3,100.

Nordiska

Verticals

Model	Size	Style and Finish	Price*
108	44"	Polished Ebony	2,780.
108	44"	Polished Walnut	2,780.
108	44"	Polished Mahogany	2,780.
116-C	46"	Polished Ebony	3,180.
116-C	46"	Polished Walnut	3,180.
116-C	46"	Polished Mahogany	3,180.
116-CB	46"	Chippendale Polished Ebony	3,580.
116-CB	46"	Chippendale Polished Walnut	3,580.
116-CB	46"	Chippendale Polished Mahogany	3,580.
122-C	48"	Polished Ebony	3,780.
122-C	48"	Polished Walnut	3,780.
122-C	48"	Polished Mahogany	3,780.

Grands

Model	Size	Style and Finish	Price*
165	5' 5"	Polished Ebony	10,190.

Pearl River

Where not specifically listed, any model can be special-ordered in white.

Verticals

Model	Size	Style and Finish	Price*
UP-108T	43"	Continental Polished Ebony	2,950.
UP-108T	43"	Continental Polished Medium Walnut	2,950.
UP-108T	43"	Continental Pol. Burgundy Mahogany	2,950.
UP-108T	43"	Continental Polished Brown Mahogany	2,950.
UP-108T	43"	Continental Polished White	2,950.
UP-108B	43"	Continental Polished Ebony	2,870.
UP-108B	43"	Continental Polished Medium Walnut	2,870.
UP-108B	43"	Continental Pol. Burgundy Mahogany	2,870.
UP-108B	43"	Continental Polished Brown Mahogany	2,870.

Model	Size	Style and Finish	Price*
UP-108B	43"	Continental Polished White	2,870.
UP-108B	43"	*Above models with European veneer*	3,070.
UP-108M	43"	Polished Ebony	2,870.
UP-108M	43"	Polished Medium Walnut	2,870.
UP-108M	43"	Polished Burgundy Mahogany	2,870.
UP-108M	43"	Polished Brown Mahogany	2,870.
UP-108M	43"	*Above models with oak veneer*	3,070.
UP-108M-2	43"	Chippendale Polished Ebony	2,950.
UP-108M-2	43"	Chippendale Polished Medium Walnut	2,950.
UP-108M-2	43"	Chippendale Pol. Burgundy Mahogany	2,950.
UP-108M-2	43"	Chippendale Polished Brown Mahogany	2,950.
UP-110P-2	43"	Chippendale Mahogany	3,470.
UP-110P-2	43"	Chippendale Medium Walnut	3,470.
UP-110P-2	43"	Chippendale Brown Mahogany	3,470.
UP-110R	43"	Walnut	3,470.
UP-110R	43"	Mahogany	3,470.
UP-110R-1	44"	Brown Mahogany	3,670.
UP-110R-1	44"	Cherry Mahogany	3,670.
UP-110R-1	44"	Medium Walnut	3,670.
UP-114B	45"	Continental Polished Ebony	2,990.
UP-114B	45"	Continental Polished Medium Walnut	2,990.
UP-114B	45"	Continental Polished Brown Mahogany	2,990.
UP-115M-3	45"	Deluxe Polished Ebony	3,190.
UP-115M-3	45"	Deluxe Medium Walnut	3,190.
UP-115M-3	45"	Deluxe Brown Mahogany	3,190.
UP-118M-2	46"	Chippendale Polished Ebony	3,390.
UP-118M-2	46"	Chippendale Polished Medium Walnut	3,390.
UP-118M-2	46"	Chippendale Pol. Burgundy Mahogany	3,390.
UP-118M-2	46"	Chippendale Polished Brown Mahogany	3,390.
UP-118M-4	46"	Deluxe Polished Ebony	3,390.
UP-118M-4	46"	Deluxe Polished Medium Walnut	3,390.
UP-118M-4	46"	Deluxe Polished Burgundy Mahogany	3,390.
UP-118M-4	46"	Deluxe Polished Brown Mahogany	3,390.
UP-120M	48"	Deluxe Polished Ebony	3,590.
UP-120M	48"	Deluxe Polished Medium Walnut	3,590.
UP-120M	48"	Deluxe Polished Burgundy Mahogany	3,590.
UP-120M	48"	Deluxe Polished Brown Mahogany	3,590.

*For explanation of terms and prices, please see pages 45–50.

Model	Size	Style and Finish	Price*

Pearl River (continued)

UP-120M-1	48"	Deluxe Polished Ebony/Oak	3,990.
UP-120M-1	48"	Deluxe Polished Green/Oak	3,990.
UP-120M-2	48"	Chippendale Cherry Mahogany	4,190.
UP-125M	49"	Deluxe Polished Ebony	4,350.
UP-125M	49"	Deluxe Polished Medium Walnut	4,350.
UP-125M	49"	Deluxe Polished Burgundy Mahogany	4,350.
UP-125M	49"	Deluxe Polished Brown Mahogany	4,350.
UP-125M-1	49"	Polished Ebony	4,590.
UP-125P-1	49"	Polished Antique White with Gold Trim	4,590.
UP-130M	51"	Polished Ebony	3,670.
UP-130M	51"	Polished Medium Walnut	3,670.
UP-130M	51"	Polished Burgundy Mahogany	3,670.
UP-130M-1	51"	Chippendale Polished Ebony	3,990.
UP-130M-1	51"	Chippendale Polished Medium Walnut	3,990.
UP-130M-1	51"	Chippendale Pol. Burgundy Mahogany	3,990.
UP-130T	51"	Deluxe Polished Ebony	4,550.
UP-130T	51"	Deluxe Polished Medium Walnut	4,550.
UP-130T	51"	Deluxe Polished Brown Mahogany	4,550.
UP-130T-2	51"	Deluxe Designer Panel Polished Ebony	5,100.
UP-130T-2	51"	Deluxe Designer Panel Pol. Burg. Mah.	5,100.
UP-130T-2	51"	Deluxe Designer Panel Pol. Brown Mah.	5,100.

Grands

GP-159	5' 2-1/2"	Polished Ebony	9,390.
GP-159	5' 2-1/2"	Polished Medium Walnut	9,590.
GP-159	5' 2-1/2"	Polished Burgundy Mahogany	9,590.
GP-159	5' 2-1/2"	Polished Brown Mahogany	9,590.
GP-159	5' 2-1/2"	Polished White	9,590.
GP-159A	5' 2-1/2"	Round Leg Polished Ebony	9,590.
GP-159A	5' 2-1/2"	Round Leg Polished Medium Walnut	9,790.
GP-159A	5' 2-1/2"	Round Leg Pol. Burgundy Mahogany	9,790.
GP-159A	5' 2-1/2"	Round Leg Polished Brown Mahogany	9,790.
GP-159A	5' 2-1/2"	Polished White	9,790.
GP-213	7'	Polished Ebony	17,990.
GP-213	7'	Polished Medium Walnut	18,190.
GP-213	7'	Polished Brown Mahogany	18,190.
GP-275	9'	Polished Ebony	44,095.
		with Renner action, add	400.

Petrof

Note: Prices below do not include bench. Add from $220 to $630 (most are under $400), depending on choice of bench.

Verticals

Model	Size	Style and Finish	Price*
100-B	42"	Barok Polished Walnut	6,100.
100-B	42"	Barok Polished Flame Mahogany	6,100.
115-I	45"	Demi-Chippendale Polished Ebony	5,700.
115-I	45"	Demi-Chippendale Polished Walnut	5,700.
115-I	45"	Demi-Chippendale Pol. Flame Mahog.	5,700.
115-IC	45"	Chippendale Polished Ebony	5,980.
115-IC	45"	Chippendale Polished Walnut	5,980.
115-IC	45"	Chippendale Polished Flame Mahogany	5,980.
115-II	45"	Continental Polished Ebony	5,180.
115-II	45"	Continental Polished Walnut	5,180.
115-II	45"	Continental Polished Flame Mahogany	5,180.
115-II	45"	Continental Polished Oak	5,180.
115-IID	45"	Polished Ebony	5,700.
115-IID	45"	Polished Walnut	5,700.
115-IID	45"	Polished Flame Mahogany	5,700.
115-V	45"	Polished Ebony	5,700.
115-V	45"	Polished Walnut	5,700.
115-V	45"	Polished Flame Mahogany	5,700.
115-VI	45"	Polished Ebony	5,500.
115-VI	45"	Polished Walnut	5,500.
115-VI	45"	Polished Flame Mahogany	5,500.
115-VII	45"	Polished Burl Walnut Veneer	5,700.
125-III	50"	Polished Walnut	6,580.
125-III	50"	Polished Flame Mahogany	6,580.
125-IV	50"	Polished Ebony	6,780.
126	50"	Polished Ebony with Walnut trim	6,980.
126 EL	50"	"Elegante" Pol. Ebony with Walnut/Gold	7,180.
131	52"	Polished Ebony	9,380.
131	52"	Polished Walnut	9,380.
131	52"	Polished Flame Mahogany	9,380.

*For explanation of terms and prices, please see pages 45–50.

Petrof (continued)

Grands

Model	Size	Style and Finish	Price*
V	5' 3"	Polished Ebony	17,180.
V	5' 3"	Polished Walnut	17,180.
V	5' 3"	Polished Flame Mahogany	17,180.
V	5' 3"	Demi-Chippendale Polished Ebony	19,180.
V	5' 3"	Demi-Chippendale Polished Walnut	19,180.
V	5' 3"	Demi-Chippendale Pol. Flame Mahog.	19,180.
IV	5' 8"	Polished Ebony	18,380.
IV	5' 8"	Polished Walnut	18,380.
IV	5' 8"	Polished Flame Mahogany	18,380.
IV	5' 8"	Demi-Chippendale Polished Ebony	20,380.
IV	5' 8"	Demi-Chippendale Polished Walnut	20,380.
IV	5' 8"	Demi-Chippendale Pol. Flame Mahog.	20,380.
IV C	5' 8"	Chippendale Polished Ebony	23,180.
IV C	5' 8"	Chippendale Polished Walnut	23,180.
IV C	5' 8"	Chippendale Polished Flame Mahogany	23,180.
III	6' 4"	Polished Ebony	21,980.
III	6' 4"	Polished Walnut	21,980.
III	6' 4"	Polished Flame Mahogany	21,980.
III M	6' 4"	"Master" Polished Ebony	30,780.
II	7' 9"	"Symphony" Polished Ebony	33,580.
I	9' 3"	"Mondial" Polished Ebony	42,780.

PianoDisc

Note: "PianoDisc" pianos have been discontinued. See under "Knabe."

Prices for PianoDisc and QuietTime systems vary by piano manufacturer and installer. The following are suggested retail prices from PianoDisc. The usual dealer discounts may apply, especially as an incentive to purchase a piano.

PDS 128 Plus System, "factory-installed" or retrofitted:

Playback only	5,199.
Add for SymphonyPro Sound Module	1,299.
Add for TFT MIDI Record system	1,299.
Add for amplified speakers, pair	749.
Add for MX Music Expansion	999.

Model	Size	Style and Finish	Price*
		Add for ProControl RF Remote	599.
		Add for PianoCD Drive	1,299.
PianoCD System			4,899.
PianoDigital QuietTime System:			
		GT-360	2,699.
		Combo with PDS 128 Plus	7,699.
		GT-90	2,099.
		Combo with PDS 128 Plus	7,199.
MIDI Controller (TFT MIDI Strip and MIDI interface board)			1,799.

Pleyel

Verticals

Model	Size	Style and Finish	Price*
Académie	45"	Polished Ebony	10,640.
Académie	45"	Polished White	10,920.
P118	47"	Polished Ebony	12,320.
P118	47"	Polished Ebony with Cherry Decor	12,880.
P118	47"	Polished Mahogany	13,720.
P118	47"	Walnut with Marquetry	12,600.
P118	47"	Cherry with Marquetry	12,600.
P118	47"	Polished White	12,600.
P124	49"	Polished Ebony	13,720.
P124	49"	Polished Mahogany	14,000.
P124	49"	Polished White	14,000.
P130	51"	Polished Ebony	15,680.
P130	51"	Add for Sostenuto	728.
P130	51"	Add for Kluge Keys	1,120.

Grands

Model	Size	Style and Finish	Price*
P190	6' 3"	Polished Ebony	39,200.
P190	6' 3"	Polished White	40,600.
P190	6' 3"	Polished Ivory	40,600.

QRS / Pianomation

Prices for Pianomation systems vary by piano manufacturer and installer. The following are suggested retail prices from QRS. The usual dealer discounts may apply, especially as an incentive to purchase a piano.

*For explanation of terms and prices, please see pages 45–50.

Model	Size	Style and Finish	Price*

QRS / Pianomation (continued)

Model	Size	Style and Finish	Price*
Pianomation:		"Piano Solo" (CD-ROM *or* 3.5" floppy)	4,700.
		Add for Orchestration option	500.
		Add for standard Record option	1,100.
		Add for optical Record option	1,800.
		Less for customer-supplied CD player	300.
		Add for both CD-ROM *and* 3.5" floppy	900.
Playola:		Playola with Orchestration, speakers, amplifier, and carrying case	6,200.
Lite Switch:		MIDI strip, mute rail, tone generator	1,395.

Ridgewood

Verticals

Model	Size	Style and Finish	Price*
108D	43"	Continental Polished Ebony	2,990.
108D	43"	Continental Polished Mahogany	3,050.
108D	43"	Continental Polished Walnut	3,050.
108D	43"	Continental Polished White	3,070.
108M	43"	Polished Ebony	3,090.
108M	43"	Polished Mahogany	3,130.
108M	43"	Polished Walnut	3,130.
108M2	43"	Chippendale Polished Ebony	3,210.
108M2	43"	Chippendale Polished Mahogany	3,000.
108M2	43"	Chippendale Polished Walnut	3,000.
108M2	43"	Chippendale Polished White	3,270.
110	43"	French Provincial Cherry	3,700.
110	43"	Walnut	3,700.
110	43"	Light Walnut	3,700.
110	43"	Mahogany	3,700.
118M2	45-1/2"	Chippendale Polished Mahogany	3,680.
118M4	45-1/2"	Polished Ebony	3,790.
118M4	45-1/2"	Polished Mahogany	3,850.

Grands

Model	Size	Style and Finish	Price*
159	5' 2"	Polished Ebony	9,590.
159	5' 2"	Polished Mahogany	9,790.
159	5' 2"	Polished Walnut	9,790.
159	5' 2"	Polished White	9,790.
159	5' 2"	Deluxe Polished Walnut	10,190.
213	7'	Polished Ebony	17,800.

Model	Size	Style and Finish	Price*

Rieger-Kloss — see "Bohemia / Rieger-Kloss"

Rösler

Verticals

Model	Size	Style and Finish	Price*
113-VIII	45"	Ebony	3,790.
113-VIII	45"	Walnut	3,790.
113-VIII	45"	Natural Oak	3,790.
113-VIII	45"	Black Oak	3,790.

Sagenhaft

Verticals

Model	Size	Style and Finish	Price*
S-111	44-1/2"	Continental Polished Ebony	2,590.
S-111	44-1/2"	Continental Polished Walnut	2,690.
S-111	44-1/2"	Continental Polished Mahogany	2,690.
S-112	44-1/2"	Deluxe Continental Polished Ebony	2,660.
S-112	44-1/2"	Deluxe Continental Polished Walnut	2,760.
S-112	44-1/2"	Deluxe Continental Polished Mahogany	2,760.
S-115L	44-1/2"	Polished Ebony	2,990.
S-115L	44-1/2"	Polished Walnut	3,090.
S-115L	44-1/2"	Polished Mahogany	3,090.
S-116C	45-1/2"	Continental Polished Ebony	3,390.
S-116C	45-1/2"	Continental Polished Walnut	3,490.
S-116S	45-1/2"	Chippendale Polished Ebony	3,490.
S-116S	45-1/2"	Chippendale Polished Mahogany	3,590.
S-116CA	45-1/2"	Baroque Polished Ebony	3,990.
S-116CA	45-1/2"	Baroque Polished Mahogany	4,090.
S-121L	48"	Polished Ebony	3,390.
S-121L	48"	Polished Walnut	3,490.
S-126L	50"	Polished Ebony	3,790.

Grands

Model	Size	Style and Finish	Price*
SG-165	5' 6"	Polished Ebony	9,990.

*For explanation of terms and prices, please see pages 45–50.

Model	Size	Style and Finish	Price*

Samick

Verticals

Model	Size	Style and Finish	Price*
SU-108P	42"	Continental Polished Ebony	3,590.
SU-108P	42"	Continental Walnut	3,790.
SU-108P	42"	Continental Polished Walnut	3,790.
SU-108P	42"	Continental Polished Mahogany	3,790.
SU-108P	42"	Continental Oak	3,790.
SU-108P	42"	Continental Polished Oak	3,790.
SU-108P	42"	Continental Polished Ivory	3,590.
SU-108P	42"	Continental Polished White	3,590.
JS 108	43"	Continental Polished Ebony	2,990.
JS 108	43"	Continental Walnut	2,790.
JS 108	43"	Continental Polished Walnut	3,090.
JS 108	43"	Continental Polished Mahogany	3,090.
JS 108	43"	Continental Polished Ivory	3,090.
JS 108	43"	Continental Polished White	3,090.
JS 043M	43"	Mediterranean Brown Oak	3,290.
JS 043F	43"	French Provincial Brown Oak	3,390.
JS 043F	43"	French Provincial Cherry	3,390.
JS 112	44"	Polished Ebony	3,190.
JS 112	44"	Walnut	2,990.
JS 112	44"	Polished Walnut	3,290.
JS 112	44"	Polished Mahogany	3,290.
JS 112	44"	Polished Ivory	3,290.
JS 112	44"	Polished White	3,290.
SU-147S	46-1/2"	Ebony	4,390.
SU-147S	46-1/2"	Polished Ebony	4,390.
SU-147S	46-1/2"	Walnut	4,590.
SU-147S	46-1/2"	Polished Walnut	4,590.
SU-147S	46-1/2"	Mahogany	4,590.
SU-147S	46-1/2"	Polished Mahogany	4,590.
SU-147S	46-1/2"	Oak	4,590.
SU-147S	46-1/2"	Polished Oak	4,590.
SU-118FA	46-1/2"	French Polished Walnut	5,190.
SU-118FA	46-1/2"	French Polished Mahogany	5,190.
JS 118M	46-1/2"	Mediterranean Brown Oak	3,790.

Model	Size	Style and Finish	Price*
JS 118F	46-1/2"	French Provincial Brown Oak	3,990.
JS 118F	46-1/2"	French Provincial Cherry	3,990.
JS 118T	46-1/2"	Mahogany	3,990.
JS 118T	46-1/2"	Cherry	3,990.
SU-121B	48"	Ebony	4,590.
SU-121B	48"	Polished Ebony	4,590.
SU-121B	48"	Walnut	4,790.
SU-121B	48"	Polished Walnut	4,790.
SU-121B	48"	Mahogany	4,790.
SU-121B	48"	Polished Mahogany	4,790.
JS 121F	48"	French Provincial Polished Ebony	3,990.
JS 121F	48"	French Provincial Polished Mahogany	4,390.
WSV-121LD	48"	Ebony	5,190.
WSV-121LD	48"	Polished Ebony	5,190.
WSV-121LD	48"	Mahogany	5,390.
WSV-121LD	48"	Polished Mahogany	5,390.
SU-131B	52"	Ebony	5,390.
SU-131B	52"	Polished Ebony	5,390.
SU-131B	52"	Walnut	5,590.
SU-131B	52"	Polished Walnut	5,590.
SU-131B	52"	Mahogany	5,590.
SU-131B	52"	Polished Mahogany	5,590.
WSV-131GD	52"	Ebony	5,990.
WSV-131GD	52"	Polished Ebony	5,990.
WSV-131GD	52"	Mahogany	6,390.
WSV-131GD	52"	Polished Mahogany	6,390.

Grands

Model	Size	Style and Finish	Price*
SIG 50	4' 11-1/2"	Polished Ebony	7,390.
SIG 50	4' 11-1/2"	Polished Ivory	7,390.
SIG 50	4' 11-1/2"	Polished White	7,390.
SG-150C	4' 11-1/2"	Ebony	9,190.
SG-150C	4' 11-1/2"	Polished Ebony	9,190.
SG-150C	4' 11-1/2"	Walnut	9,590.
SG-150C	4' 11-1/2"	Polished Walnut	9,590.
SG-150C	4' 11-1/2"	Mahogany	9,590.
SG-150C	4' 11-1/2"	Polished Mahogany	9,590.
SG-150C	4' 11-1/2"	Oak	9,590.

*For explanation of terms and prices, please see pages 45–50.

Model	Size	Style and Finish	Price*

Samick (continued)

Model	Size	Style and Finish	Price*
SG-150C	4' 11-1/2"	Polished Oak	9,590.
SG-150C	4' 11-1/2"	Cherry	9,590.
SG-150C	4' 11-1/2"	Polished Ivory	9,390.
SG-150C	4' 11-1/2"	Polished White	9,390.
SG-150KAF	4' 11-1/2"	French Provincial (all of above finishes)	11,190.
SG-150KBF	4' 11-1/2"	French Provincial (all of above finishes)	11,590.
SG-161	5' 3-1/2"	Ebony	10,390.
SG-161	5' 3-1/2"	Polished Ebony	10,390.
SG-161	5' 3-1/2"	Walnut	10,790.
SG-161	5' 3-1/2"	Polished Walnut	10,790.
SG-161	5' 3-1/2"	Mahogany	10,790.
SG-161	5' 3-1/2"	Polished Mahogany	10,790.
SG-161	5' 3-1/2"	Oak	10,790.
SG-161	5' 3-1/2"	Polished Oak	10,790.
SG-161	5' 3-1/2"	Cherry	10,790.
SG-161	5' 3-1/2"	Polished Ivory	10,590.
SG-161	5' 3-1/2"	Polished White	10,590.
SG-161KAF	5' 3-1/2"	French Provincial (all of above finishes)	11,990.
SG-161KBF	5' 3-1/2"	French Provincial (all of above finishes)	12,390.
SG-172	5' 7"	Ebony	11,190.
SG-172	5' 7"	Polished Ebony	11,190.
SG-172	5' 7"	Walnut	11,590.
SG-172	5' 7"	Polished Walnut	11,590.
SG-172	5' 7"	Mahogany	11,590.
SG-172	5' 7"	Polished Mahogany	11,590.
SG-172	5' 7"	Oak	11,590.
SG-172	5' 7"	Polished Oak	11,590.
SG-172	5' 7"	Cherry	11,590.
SG-172	5' 7"	Polished Ivory	11,390.
SG-172	5' 7"	Polished White	11,390.
SG-172L	5' 7"	Empire Ebony	12,190.
SG-172L	5' 7"	Empire Polished Ebony	12,190.
SG-172L	5' 7"	Empire Mahogany	12,590.
SG-172L	5' 7"	Empire Polished Mahogany	12,590.
SG-185	6' 1"	Ebony	11,990.
SG-185	6' 1"	Polished Ebony	11,990.

Model	Size	Style and Finish	Price*
SG-185	6' 1"	*Walnut*	12,590.
SG-185	6' 1"	*Polished Walnut*	12,590.
SG-185	6' 1"	*Mahogany*	12,590.
SG-185	6' 1"	*Polished Mahogany*	12,590.
SG-185	6' 1"	*Oak*	12,590.
SG-185	6' 1"	*Polished Oak*	12,590.
SG-185	6' 1"	*Polished Ivory*	12,590.
SG-185	6' 1"	*Polished White*	12,590.
SG-185L	6' 1"	Empire Ebony	12,990.
SG-185L	6' 1"	Empire Polished Ebony	12,990.
SG-185L	6' 1"	Empire Mahogany	13,590.
SG-185L	6' 1"	Empire Polished Mahogany	13,590.
WFG-185	6' 1"	Ebony	17,500.
WFG-185	6' 1"	Polished Ebony	17,500.
WFG-185	6' 1"	*All other finishes (see SG-185)*	17,900.
WFG-185L	6' 1"	Empire Ebony	18,500.
WFG-185L	6' 1"	Empire Polished Ebony	18,500.
WFG-185L	6' 1"	Empire Mahogany	18,900.
WFG-185L	6' 1"	Empire Polished Mahogany	18,900.
WFG-205	6' 8"	Ebony	19,990.
WFG-205	6' 8"	Polished Ebony	19,990.
WFG-205	6' 8"	*All other finishes (see SG-185)*	20,390.
WFG-225	7' 4"	Ebony	25,400.
WFG-225	7' 4"	Polished Ebony	25,400.
WFG-225	7' 4"	*All other finishes (see SG-185)*	25,800.
WFG-275	9' 1"	Ebony	45,990.
WFG-275	9' 1"	Polished Ebony	45,990.
WFG-275	9' 1"	*All other finishes (see SG-185)*	47,990.

Sängler & Söhne / Wieler

Verticals

Model	Size	Style and Finish	Price*
UP-108	43"	Continental Polished Ebony	2,500.
UP-108	43"	Continental Polished Mahogany	2,500.
UP-108	43"	Continental Polished Walnut	2,500.
UP-108	43"	Continental Polished White	2,500.
UP-108M2	43"	Chippendale Polished Ebony	2,750.
UP-108M2	43"	Chippendale Polished Brown Mahogany	2,750.

*For explanation of terms and prices, please see pages 45–50.

Model	Size	Style and Finish	Price*

Sängler & Söhne (continued)

Model	Size	Style and Finish	Price*
UP-110P	44"	French Provincial Polished Mahogany	2,990.
UP-110P	44"	French Provincial Polished Walnut	2,990.
UP-110R	44"	Fruitwood	2,990.
UP-110R	44"	Mahogany	2,990.
UP-115M	45"	Polished Ebony	2,790.
UP-115M	45"	Polished Brown Mahogany	2,790.
BLR-120	47"	Continental Polished Ebony	1,990.
BLR-120	47"	Continental Polished Mahogany	1,990.

Grands

GP-159	5' 3"	Polished Ebony	8,590.

Sauter

These pianos are purchased by the dealer directly from Sauter in Germany. The prices below are FOB Germany and so do not include duty, freight, and other costs of importing.

Verticals

112	44"	"Carus" Ebony or Polished Ebony	8,227.
112	44"	"Nova" Ebony	9,625.
112	44"	"Nova" Polished Ebony	10,705.
112	44"	"Nova" Mahogany, Walnut, or Oak	9,625.
112	44"	"Nova" Cherry	10,216.
112	44"	"Nova" Polished White	10,920.
112	44"	"Schulpiano" Oak, Walnut, or Beech	9,091.
114	45"	"Andiamo" Polished Ebony	10,318.
114	45"	"Andiamo" Mahogany, Walnut, or Oak	9,591.
114	45"	"Andiamo" Cherry	10,068.
114	45"	"Andiamo" Cherry/Yew	10,318.
114	45"	"Andiamo" Beech or Waxed Beech	9,625.
114	45"	"Andiamo" Alder	9,591.
114	45"	"Andiamo" Polished White	10,636.
114	45"	"Ragazza" Polished Ebony	10,636.
114	45"	"Ragazza" French Walnut	10,318.
114	45"	"Ragazza" Waxed Beech or Alder	10,636.
114	45"	"Ragazza" Polished White	10,920.

Model	Size	Style and Finish	Price*
120	47"	"Premiere" Ebony	10,830.
120	47"	"Premiere" Polished Ebony	11,750.
120	47"	"Premiere" Mahogany, Walnut, or Oak	10,830.
120	47"	"Premiere" Polished Mahogany	12,727.
120	47"	"Premiere" Cherry	11,341.
120	47"	"Premiere" Cherry/Yew	11,750.
120	47"	"Premiere" Alder	11,011.
120	47"	"Premiere" Polished White	12,205.
122	48"	"Avenue" Waxed Alder	12,557.
122	48"	"Barock" Polished Ebony	14,807.
122	48"	"Barock" Walnut	14,034.
122	48"	"Barock" Cherry	14,295.
122	48"	Chippendale Walnut	13,943.
122	48"	"Domino" Polished Ebony	12,125.
122	48"	"Domino" Pear	12,057.
122	48"	"Domino" Beech	11,534.
122	48"	"Domino" Maple	11,705.
122	48"	"M-Line 2" Polished Ebony	15,591.
122	48"	"Ragazza" Pol. Ebony or Pol. Steel-Blue	12,216.
122	48"	"Resonance" Ebony	12,500.
122	48"	"Resonance" Polished Ebony	13,352.
122	48"	"Resonance" Walnut, Oak, or Pine	12,648.
122	48"	"Resonance" Cherry	12,920.
122	48"	"Resonance" Cherry/Yew	13,284.
122	48"	"Schulpiano" Oak, Walnut, or Beech	9,864.
122	48"	"True-Love" French Walnut	13,216.
122	48"	"True-Love" Yew	14,182.
122	48"	"True-Love" Polished Yew	14,886.
122	48"	"Vista" Polished Ebony	12,795.
122	48"	"Vista" Beech	12,216.
122	48"	"Vista" Maple	11,875.
122	48"	"Vista" Pear	12,727.
Peter Maly	48"	"Artes" Polished Ebony	18,341.
Peter Maly	48"	"Artes" Polished White	18,750.
Peter Maly	48"	"Cura" Cherry or Pine	16,716.
Peter Maly	48"	"Imago" Swiss Pear/Grey	15,625.
Peter Maly	48"	"Imago" Cherry/Blue or Maple/White	15,625.
Peter Maly	48"	"Onda" Maple/Silver or Beech	12,443.

*For explanation of terms and prices, please see pages 45–50.

Model	Size	Style and Finish	Price*

Sauter (continued)

Model	Size	Style and Finish	Price*
128	50"	"M-Line 1" Polished Ebony	18,125.
130	51"	"Competence" Polished Ebony	14,886.
130	51"	"Competence" Walnut	14,045.
130	51"	"Competence" Polished White	15,159.
Grands			
160	5' 3"	"Alpha" Polished Ebony	31,170.
160	5' 3"	"Alpha" Mahogany, Oak, or Walnut	27,693.
160	5' 3"	Chippendale Mahogany, Oak, or Walnut	30,057.
160	5' 3"	"Noblesse" Mahogany, Oak, or Walnut	32,523.
160	5' 3"	"Noblesse" Pol. Mahog., Oak, or Walnut	36,784.
160	5' 3"	"Noblesse" Cherry	33,489.
160	5' 3"	"Noblesse" Polished Cherry	37,773.
185	6' 1"	Chippendale Mahogany, Oak, or Walnut	32,602.
185	6' 1"	"Delta" Polished Ebony	34,023.
185	6' 1"	"Delta" Mahogany, Oak, or Walnut	30,545.
185	6' 1"	"Delta" Polished White	34,932.
185	6' 1"	"Noblesse" Mahogany, Oak, or Walnut	35,080.
185	6' 1"	"Noblesse" Pol. Mahog., Oak, or Walnut	39,466.
185	6' 1"	"Noblesse" Cherry	36,091.
185	6' 1"	"Noblesse" Polished Cherry	40,477.
Peter Maly	6' 1"	"Vivace" Polished Ebony	47,136.
Peter Maly	6' 1"	"Vivace" Maple	43,852.
Peter Maly	6' 1"	"Vivace" Polished White	47,977.
220	7' 3"	"Omega" Polished Ebony	43,159.
220	7' 3"	"Omega" Mahogany, Oak, or Walnut	39,670.

Schimmel

The models and finishes listed below are the ones most frequently imported into the U.S. The Schimmel catalog shows many additional models and finishes, which are available by special order.

Verticals

Model	Size	Style and Finish	Price*
112 S	45"	Open-Pore Walnut	12,580.
112 S	45"	Open-Pore Oak	12,580.
114 K	45"	"Classicism" Polished Ebony	12,680.
116 S	46"	"Special" Polished Ebony	11,380.

Model	Size	Style and Finish	Price*
116 I	46"	"International" Polished Ebony	12,380.
120 I	48"	"International" Polished Ebony	12,880.
120 J	48"	"Centennial" Polished Mahogany	13,580.
120 LE	48"	*"Lyra Exquisite" Polished Ebony*	13,280.
120 LE	48"	"Lyra Exquisite" Polished Mahogany	13,680.
120 RI	48"	"Royale Intarsia" Polished Mahogany	15,580.
120 S	48"	Open-Pore Oak	12,980.
120 T	48"	Polished Ebony	13,080.
120 T	48"	*Polished Walnut*	13,480.
120 T	48"	*Polished Mahogany*	13,480.
120 T	48"	Polished White	13,680.
120 TN	48"	"Noblesse" Polished Ebony	13,380.
120 TN	48"	"Noblesse" Polished White	13,980.
122 KE	49"	"Classicism Exquisite" Polished Ebony	13,380.
122 KE	49"	"Classicism Exquisite" Pol. Mahogany	13,780.
125 DN	49"	"Diamond Noblesse" Polished Ebony	17,180.
125 DN	49"	"Diamond Noblesse" Polished Mahog.	17,580.
125 DP	49"	"Diamond Prestige" Polished Ebony	17,580.
125 DP	49"	"Diamond Prestige" Polished Mahogany	17,980.
130 T	51"	Polished Ebony	15,380.
130 T	51"	*Polished Walnut*	15,780.
130 T	51"	Polished Mahogany	15,780.

Grands

When not mentioned, satin finish available on special order at same price as high-polish finish.

Model	Size	Style and Finish	Price*
SP 182 C	6'	*Chippendale Polished Walnut*	38,380.
SP 182 C	6'	*Chippendale Polished Mahogany*	38,380.
SP 182 DE	6'	"Diamond" Polished Ebony	38,980.
SP 182 DE	6'	"Diamond" Polished Bubinga	47,980.
SP 182 DE	6'	"Diamond" Polished Bird's Eye Maple	47,980.
SP 182 E	6'	*Empire Polished Mahogany*	42,980.
SP 182 LE	6'	Limited Edition Polished Ebony	35,980.
SP 182 S	6'	Open-Pore Oak	33,780.
SP 182 T	6'	Ebony	34,580.
SP 182 T	6'	Polished Ebony	34,580.
SP 182 T	6'	*Polished Walnut*	35,380.
SP 182 T	6'	Polished Mahogany	35,380.

*For explanation of terms and prices, please see pages 45–50.

Model	Size	Style and Finish	Price*

Schimmel (continued)

Model	Size	Style and Finish	Price*
SP 182 T	6'	*Polished White*	35,580.
SP 182 TE	6'	"Exquisite" Polished Ebony	36,180.
SP 182 TE	6'	"Exquisite" Polished Mahogany	36,980.
SP 182 TEI	6'	"Exquisite" Intarsia Polished Mahogany	38,180.
SG 182 TJ	6'	"Jubilee" Polished Ebony	36,580.
SG 182 TJ	6'	*"Jubilee" Polished Cherry*	37,180.
SG 182 TJ	6'	"Jubilee" Polished Mahogany	37,580.
CC 208 A	6' 10"	*Art Edition*	117,800.
CC 208 DE	6' 10"	"Diamond" Polished Ebony	43,980.
CC 208 DE	6' 10"	"Diamond" Polished Bubinga	47,980.
CC 208 DE	6' 10"	"Diamond" Polished Bird's Eye Maple	47,980.
CC 208 G	6' 10"	*Plexiglas (any color)*	97,800.
CC 208 P	6' 10"	*"Pegasus" (any color)*	169,800.
CC 208 S	6' 10"	Open-Pore Oak	37,780.
CC 208 T	6' 10"	*Ebony*	38,980.
CC 208 T	6' 10"	Polished Ebony	38,980.
CC 208 T	6' 10"	*Walnut*	39,780.
CC 208 T	6' 10"	*Polished Walnut*	39,780.
CC 208 T	6' 10"	*Mahogany*	39,780.
CC 208 T	6' 10"	*Polished Mahogany*	39,780.
CC 208 T	6' 10"	*Polished White*	39,980.
CO 256 T	8' 4"	Polished Ebony	59,800.

Schirmer & Son

Verticals

Model	Size	Style and Finish	Price*
M-105 C	42"	Continental Polished Ebony	4,590.
M-105 C	42"	Continental Polished Mahogany	4,590.
M-113 D	44"	Polished Ebony	5,790.
M-118 A	47"	Polished Ebony	5,990.
M-118 A	47"	Polished Mahogany	5,990.
M-118 A	47"	Polished Walnut	5,990.
M-118 A	47"	Polished Cherry	5,990.
M-118 CH	47"	Chippendale Polished Ebony	6,190.
M-118 CH	47"	Chippendale Polished Mahogany	6,190.
M-118 CH	47"	Chippendale Polished Walnut	6,190.

Model	Size	Style and Finish	Price*
M-118 CH	47"	Chippendale Polished White	6,590.
M-128 E	51"	Polished Ebony	6,790.
M-128 E	51"	Polished Mahogany	6,790.
M-128 E	51"	Polished Walnut	6,790.
Grands			
M-163 S	5' 4"	Polished Ebony	15,990.
M-190 S	6' 3"	Polished Ebony	19,990.
M-190 CH	6' 3"	Chippendale Polished Ebony	23,990.
M-273 S	9'	Polished Ebony	35,990.

Schubert

Verticals

B-16	43"	Continental Polished Ebony	2,258.
B-16	43"	Continental Polished Mahogany	2,258.
B-16	43"	Continental Polished Walnut	2,258
B-16	43"	Continental Polished Oak	2,258.
B-17	44"	American Oak	2,390.
B-17	44"	Country French Oak	2,450.
B-17	44"	French Provincial Mahogany	2,450.
B-18	44"	Polished Ebony	2,490.
B-18	44"	Polished Mahogany	2,490.
B-18	44"	Polished Walnut	2,490.
B-18	44"	Oak	2,490.
B-18	44"	Polished Oak	2,490.
B-19	44"	Chippendale Polished Ebony	2,590.
B-19	44"	Chippendale Polished Mahogany	2,590.
B-19	44"	Chippendale Polished Walnut	2,590.
B-19	44"	Chippendale Polished Oak	2,590.
B-19	44"	Chippendale Polished Cherry	2,590.
B-15	47"	Polished Ebony	2,598.
B-15	47"	Polished Mahogany	2,598.
B-15	47"	Polished Walnut	2,598.
B-15	47"	Polished Oak	2,598.
B-15	47"	Polished Cherry	2,598.

*For explanation of terms and prices, please see pages 45–50.

Model	Size	Style and Finish	Price*

Schultz & Sons

Model numbers beginning with 3 or 4 designate pianos manufactured by Broadwood, numbers beginning with 7 or 8, by Samick.

Verticals

Model	Size	Style and Finish	Price
7507-C	43-1/2"	Polished Ebony	4,880.
7507-C	43-1/2"	Polished Walnut	4,972.
7507-C	43-1/2"	Polished Mahogany	4,972.
7507-C	43-1/2"	Polished White	4,972.
3801-C	44"	Polished Ebony	14,882.
3801-C	44"	Mahogany	13,994.
3801-C	44"	Polished Mahogany	15,994.
3801-C	44"	Walnut	13,994.
3801-C	44"	Polished Walnut	15,994.
7505-S	46-1/2"	Brown Oak	5,862.
7505-S	46-1/2"	Cherry	5,862.
7505-S	46-1/2"	French Provincial Cherry	6,018.
3807-S	47"	Polished Ebony	16,676.
3807-S	47"	Mahogany	15,786.
3807-S	47"	Polished Mahogany	17,786.
3807-S	47"	Walnut	15,786.
3807-S	47"	Polished Walnut	17,786.
3809-S	47"	Mahogany	19,034.
3809-S	47"	Polished Mahogany	19,922.
7609-S	48"	Polished Ebony	6,064.
7609-S	48"	Polished Mahogany	6,372.
3817-U	50"	Polished Ebony	21,840.
3817-U	50"	Mahogany	20,952.
3817-U	50"	Polished Mahogany	22,952.
3817-U	50"	Walnut	20,952.
3817-U	50"	Polished Walnut	22,952.
7711-U	52"	Polished Ebony	7,628.
7711-U	52"	Polished Mahogany	7,888.

Grands

Model	Size	Style and Finish	Price
8401-B	4' 11-1/2"	Polished Ebony	11,696.
8401-B	4' 11-1/2"	Polished Ivory	11,696.
8401-B	4' 11-1/2"	Polished White	11,696.

Model	Size	Style and Finish	Price*
8501-B	5' 3-1/2"	Polished Ebony	14,266.
8501-B	5' 3-1/2"	Polished Walnut	14,944.
8501-B	5' 3-1/2"	Polished Mahogany	14,944.
8501-B	5' 3-1/2"	Polished Ivory	14,266.
8501-B	5' 3-1/2"	Polished White	14,266.
8601-M	5' 9"	Polished Ebony	15,880.
8601-M	5' 9"	Polished Mahogany	16,574.
4908-L	6'	Polished Ebony	56,772.
8701-SX	6' 10"	Polished Ebony	29,310.
8801-SX	7' 4"	Polished Ebony	40,682.

Schulze Pollmann

Verticals

117E	46"	Polished Ebony	7,960.
117E	46"	Oval Black Panel	8,200.
117E	46"	Walnut	8,700.
117E	46"	Polished Walnut	8,700.
117E	46"	Briar Walnut	8,700.
117E	46"	Polished Briar Walnut	8,700.
117E	46"	Polished Mahogany	8,700.
117E	46"	Polished Briar Mahogany	8,700.
117E	46"	Cherry	8,700.
117E	46"	Cherry/Yew	8,700.
126E	50"	Polished Ebony	9,100.
126E	50"	Oval Black Panel	9,340.
126E	50"	Oval Feather Mahogany	9,780.
126E	50"	Oval Peacock Walnut	9,780.
126E	50"	Polished Ebony with Gold Borders	9,780.
126E	50"	Walnut	9,780.
126E	50"	Polished Walnut	9,780.
126E	50"	Peacock Walnut	9,780.
126E	50"	Polished Peacock Walnut	9,780.
126E	50"	Briar Walnut	9,780.
126E	50"	Polished Briar Walnut	9,780.
126E	50"	Polished Ebony with "Masterpiece"	9,980.

*For explanation of terms and prices, please see pages 45–50.

Model	Size	Style and Finish	Price*

Schulze Pollmann (continued)

Grands

190F	6' 3"	Polished Ebony	27,900.
190F	6' 3"	Polished Mahogany	31,900.
190F	6' 3"	Polished Briar Mahogany	31,900.
190F	6' 3"	Polished Walnut	31,900.
190F	6' 3"	Polished Briar Walnut	31,900.

Seiler

Verticals

116	46"	"Favorit" Continental Open-Pore Ebony	12,940.
116	46"	"Favorit" Continental Polished Ebony	13,980.
116	46"	"Favorit" Continental Open-Pore Walnut	12,940.
116	46"	"Favorit" Continental Open-Pore Oak	12,940.
116	46"	"Favorit" Continental Polished White	14,320.
116	46"	School Open-Pore Ebony	12,940.
116	46"	School Open-Pore Oak	12,940.
116	46"	"Mondial" Open-Pore Ebony	13,300.
116	46"	"Mondial" Open-Pore Walnut	13,300.
116	46"	"Mondial" Open-Pore Mahogany	13,300.
116	46"	"Mondial" Polished Mahogany	13,980.
116	46"	"Mondial" Open-Pore Oak	13,300.
116	46"	"Mondial" Open-Pore Cherry	13,980.
116	46"	"Jubilee" Polished Ebony	14,280.
116	46"	"Jubilee" Polished White	14,506.
116	46"	Chippendale Open-Pore Walnut	13,450.
116	46"	"Escorial" Open-Pore Cherry Intarsia	14,500.
122	48"	"Konsole" Open-Pore Ebony	13,840.
122	48"	"Konsole" Polished Ebony	14,790.
122	48"	"Konsole" Open-Pore Walnut	13,840.
122	48"	"Konsole" Polished Walnut	17,100.
122	48"	"Konsole" Open-Pore Oak	13,840.
122	48"	"Konsole" Open-Pore Cherry	14,530.
122	48"	"Konsole" Polished Brown Ash	17,100.
122	48"	"Konsole" Polished White	15,160.
122	48"	School Open-Pore Ebony	13,220.

Model	Size	Style and Finish	Price*
122	48"	School Open-Pore Walnut	13,220.
122	48"	School Open-Pore Oak	13,220.
122	48"	"Vienna" Polished Ebony	15,180.
122	48"	"Vienna" Pol. Mahogany with Inlays	17,100.
122	48"	"Vienna" Polished Walnut with Inlays	17,100.
122	48"	"Vienna" Open-Pore Cherry Intarsia	15,960.
122	48"	"Bell'Arte" Open-Pore Cherry/Macassar	16,170.
122	48"	"Ars Vivendi" Polished Ebony	16,170.
131	52"	"Concert SMR" Polished Ebony	16,370.
131	52"	"Concert SMR" Open-Pore Walnut	15,400.
131	52"	"Concert SMR" Polished Mahogany	16,860.

Grands

Model	Size	Style and Finish	Price*
180	5' 11"	"Maestro" Polished Ebony	35,900.
180	5' 11"	"Maestro" Open-Pore Walnut	34,150.
180	5' 11"	"Maestro" Polished Walnut	37,250.
180	5' 11"	"Maestro" Open-Pore Mahogany	34,150.
180	5' 11"	"Maestro" Polished Mahogany	37,250.
180	5' 11"	"Maestro" Polished Pyramid Mahogany	45,720.
180	5' 11"	"Maestro" Polished Burl Rosewood	43,600.
180	5' 11"	"Maestro" Polished White	36,720.
180	5' 11"	Chippendale Open-Pore Walnut	36,820.
180	5' 11"	"Westminster" Pol. Mahogany Intarsia	48,440.
180	5' 11"	"Florenz" Pol. Walnut/Myrtle Intarsia	48,440.
180	5' 11"	"Florenz" Pol. Mahog./Myrtle Intarsia	48,440.
180	5' 11"	"Louvre" Polished Ebony	38,860.
180	5' 11"	"Louvre" Polished Cherry Intarsia	48,440.
180	5' 11"	"Louvre" Polished White	39,520.
180	5' 11"	"Prado" Polished Brown Ash	47,360.
180	5' 11"	"Prado" Polished Burl Redwood	47,360.
180	5' 11"	"Showmaster" Chrome/Brass/Polyester	96,550.
206	6' 9"	Polished Ebony	40,420.
240	8'	Polished Ebony	56,160.

*For explanation of terms and prices, please see pages 45–50.

Steck, George

The prices below include a factory-installed PianoDisc PDS 128 Plus playback system. Subtract $110 for a PianoCD system. Add $1,299 each for a SymphonyPro Sound Module or a TFT MIDI Record System. Subtract $1,800 for a factory-installed GT-360 QuietTime system instead of the PDS 128 Plus. Subtract $4,000 for a regular acoustic piano without any extra equipment.

Verticals

Model	Size	Style and Finish	Price
GSV43	43"	Light Cherry	7,890.
GSV43	43"	Dark Mahogany	7,890.

Grands

Model	Size	Style and Finish	Price
GS530	5' 3"	Polished Ebony	13,990.
GS530	5' 3"	Polished Mahogany	14,190.
GS530	5' 3"	Polished White	13,990.

Steingraeber & Söhne

This list includes only those models most likely to be offered to U.S. customers. Other models, styles, and finishes are available. "Other Woods" refers to Walnut, Oak, Beech, Alder, Maple, and at least a dozen others available by special order.

Verticals

Model	Size	Style and Finish	Price
122T	48"	Polished Ebony	21,476.
122T	48"	Cherry	22,569.
122T	48"	Polished Cherry	23,101.
122T	48"	Mahogany	22,569.
122T	48"	Polished Mahogany	23,101.
122T	48"	*Other Woods*	21,261.
122K	48"	Ebony	22,914.
122K	48"	Polished Ebony	25,861.
122K	48"	Cherry	23,618.
122K	48"	Polished Cherry	27,787.
122K	48"	Mahogany	23,618.
122K	48"	Polished Mahogany	27,787.
122K	48"	Woods with Biological Finish	29,684.
130PS	51"	Ebony	25,616.
130PS	51"	Polished Ebony	28,635.
130PS	51"	Cherry	26,349.

Model	Size	Style and Finish	Price*
130PS	51"	Polished Cherry	30,518.
130PS	51"	Mahogany	26,349.
130PS	51"	Polished Mahogany	30,518.
130PS	51"	Woods with Biological Finish	32,157.
138K	54"	Ebony	30,259.
138K	54"	Polished Ebony	31,496.
138K	54"	Cherry	34,457.
138K	54"	Polished Cherry	38,583.
138K	54"	Mahogany	34,457.
138K	54"	Polished Mahogany	38,583.
138K	54"	Woods with Biological Finish	38,482.
Grands			
168N	5' 6"	Ebony	50,054.
168N	5' 6"	Polished Ebony	51,233.
168N	5' 6"	Cherry	52,584.
168N	5' 6"	Polished Cherry	56,738.
168N	5' 6"	Mahogany	52,584.
168N	5' 6"	Polished Mahogany	56,738.
168N	5' 6"	*Other Woods*	51,262.
168N	5' 6"	Woods with Biological Finish	55,718.
168K	5' 6"	Ebony	60,634.
168K	5' 6"	Polished Ebony	60,634.
168K	5' 6"	Cherry	63,954.
168K	5' 6"	Polished Cherry	68,123.
168K	5' 6"	Mahogany	63,954.
168K	5' 6"	Polished Mahogany	68,123.
205N	6' 9"	Ebony	69,316.
205N	6' 9"	Polished Ebony	70,308.
205N	6' 9"	Cherry	72,623.
205N	6' 9"	Polished Cherry	76,878.
205N	6' 9"	Mahogany	72,623.
205N	6' 9"	Polished Mahogany	76,878.
205N	6' 9"	*Other Woods*	70,481.
205N	6' 9"	Woods with Biological Finish	75,742.

*For explanation of terms and prices, please see pages 45–50.

Steinway & Sons

Verticals

Model	Size	Style and Finish	Price*
4510	45"	Sheraton Ebony	15,400.
4510	45"	Sheraton Mahogany	17,100.
4510	45"	Sheraton Walnut	17,800.
4510	45"	Sheraton Dark Cherry	18,800.
1098	46-1/2"	Ebony	14,400.
1098	46-1/2"	Mahogany	15,700.
1098	46-1/2"	Walnut	16,400.
K-52	52"	Ebony	18,800.
K-52	52"	Mahogany	21,400.
K-52	52"	Walnut	22,100.

Grands

Model	Size	Style and Finish	Price*
S	5' 1"	Ebony	31,200.
S	5' 1"	Mahogany	35,100.
S	5' 1"	Walnut	36,500.
S	5' 1"	Figured Sapele	38,200.
S	5' 1"	Kewazinga Bubinga	39,800.
S	5' 1"	East Indian Rosewood	44,800.
S	5' 1"	Santos Rosewood	44,100.
S	5' 1"	Macassar Ebony	49,200.
S	5' 1"	Dark Cherry	38,600.
S	5' 1"	Hepplewhite Dark Cherry	40,600.
M	5' 7"	Ebony	35,900.
M	5' 7"	Mahogany	40,300.
M	5' 7"	Walnut	41,600.
M	5' 7"	Figured Sapele	43,100.
M	5' 7"	Kewazinga Bubinga	45,300.
M	5' 7"	East Indian Rosewood	50,300.
M	5' 7"	Santos Rosewood	49,600.
M	5' 7"	Macassar Ebony	55,600.
M	5' 7"	Dark Cherry	44,100.
M	5' 7"	Hepplewhite Dark Cherry	46,300.
M SK-1014A	5' 7"	Chippendale Mahogany	50,600.
M SK-1014A	5' 7"	Chippendale Walnut	51,900.
M SK-501A	5' 7"	Louis XV Walnut	65,400.
M SK-501A	5' 7"	Louis XV East Indian Rosewood	76,100.

Model	Size	Style and Finish	Price*
L	5' 10-1/2"	Ebony	40,700.
L	5' 10-1/2"	Mahogany	45,400.
L	5' 10-1/2"	Walnut	46,800.
L	5' 10-1/2"	Figured Sapele	48,600.
L	5' 10-1/2"	Kewazinga Bubinga	50,700.
L	5' 10-1/2"	East Indian Rosewood	56,800.
L	5' 10-1/2"	Santos Rosewood	55,900.
L	5' 10-1/2"	Macassar Ebony	63,100.
L	5' 10-1/2"	Dark Cherry	49,300.
L	5' 10-1/2"	Hepplewhite Dark Cherry	51,900.
L SK-390	5' 10-1/2"	"J. B. Tiffany" East Indian Rosewood	72,100.
L SK-390	5' 10-1/2"	"J. B. Tiffany" African Pommele	74,900.
B	6' 10-1/2"	Ebony	52,800.
B	6' 10-1/2"	Mahogany	58,200.
B	6' 10-1/2"	Walnut	59,800.
B	6' 10-1/2"	Figured Sapele	62,300.
B	6' 10-1/2"	Kewazinga Bubinga	65,100.
B	6' 10-1/2"	East Indian Rosewood	72,100.
B	6' 10-1/2"	Santos Rosewood	71,300.
B	6' 10-1/2"	Macassar Ebony	79,900.
B	6' 10-1/2"	Dark Cherry	63,300.
B	6' 10-1/2"	Hepplewhite Dark Cherry	66,800.
B SK-390	6' 10-1/2"	"J. B. Tiffany" East Indian Rosewood	92,600.
B SK-390	6' 10-1/2"	"J. B. Tiffany" African Pommele	97,300.
D	8' 11-3/4"	Ebony	79,900.
D	8' 11-3/4"	Mahogany	89,100.
D	8' 11-3/4"	Walnut	91,100.
D	8' 11-3/4"	Figured Sapele	96,100.
D	8' 11-3/4"	Kewazinga Bubinga	100,000.
D	8' 11-3/4"	East Indian Rosewood	110,400.
D	8' 11-3/4"	Santos Rosewood	109,700.
D	8' 11-3/4"	Macassar Ebony	122,400.
D	8' 11-3/4"	Dark Cherry	98,600.
D	8' 11-3/4"	Hepplewhite Dark Cherry	103,200.

*For explanation of terms and prices, please see pages 45–50.

Steinway & Sons (continued)

Grands (Hamburg)

I frequently get requests for prices of pianos made in Steinway's branch factory in Hamburg, Germany. Officially, these pianos are not sold in North America, but occasionally Steinway makes one available to a North American customer—usually an institution or concert hall—by special arrangement. The following list shows approximately how much it would cost to purchase a Hamburg Steinway in Germany and have it shipped to the United States. The list was derived by taking the published retail price in Germany, subtracting the value-added tax not applicable to foreign purchasers, converting to U.S. dollars (rates obviously subject to change), and adding approximate charges for duty, air freight, crating, insurance, brokerage fees, and delivery. Only prices for grands in polished ebony are shown here. *Caution:* This list is published for general informational purposes only. The price that Steinway would charge customers under the special arrangement mentioned above may be different. (Also, the cost of a trip to Germany to purchase the piano is not included!)

Model	Size	Style and Finish	Price
S-155	5' 1"	Polished Ebony	40,000.
M-170	5' 7"	Polished Ebony	43,900.
O-180	5' 10-1/2"	Polished Ebony	46,700.
A-188	6' 2"	Polished Ebony	49,900.
B-211	6' 11"	Polished Ebony	58,000.
C-227	7' 5-1/2"	Polished Ebony	68,100.
D-274	8' 11-3/4"	Polished Ebony	87,100.

Story & Clark

Factory-installed Pianomation system (CD-ROM or 3.5" floppy), add from $4,500 to $6,000, depending on options and model.

Verticals

Model	Size	Style and Finish	Price
American	42"	Oak	4,700.
American	42"	Cherry	4,700.
American	42"	Walnut	4,700.
Heirloom	42"	Queen Anne Oak	4,700.
Heirloom	42"	Queen Anne Cherry	4,700.
Heirloom	42"	Queen Anne Walnut	4,700.
Southwest	42"	French Provincial White	4,700.
Century	42"	Italian Provincial Oak	4,700.

Model	Size	Style and Finish	Price*
Century	42"	Italian Provincial Cherry	4,700.
Century	42"	Italian Provincial Walnut	4,700.
Mediterranean	42"	Mediterranean Oak	4,700.
Chippendale	42"	Chippendale Oak	4,900.
Chippendale	42"	Chippendale Cherry	4,900.
Chippendale	42"	Chippendale Walnut	4,900.
Prelude	44"	Continental Polished Ebony	2,790.
Prelude	44"	Continental Polished Mahogany	2,790.
Prelude	46"	Polished Ebony	3,390.
Prelude	46"	Polished Mahogany	3,390.
Church	46"	Ebony	4,990.
Church	46"	Oak	4,990.
Church	46"	Cherry	4,990.
Church	46"	Walnut	4,990.
School	46"	Ebony	4,990.
School	46"	Oak	4,990.
School	46"	Cherry	4,990.
School	46"	Walnut	4,990.
Cambridge	47"	"Deluxe" Ebony	3,790.
Cambridge	47"	"Deluxe" Polished Mahogany	3,790.
Cambridge	49"	"Elite" Polished Ebony	3,790.
Cambridge	54"	"Ambassador" Teak	5,990.
Cambridge	55"	"Premier" Polished Mahogany	6,390.
Grands			
47	4' 7"	Polished Ebony	10,790.
Cambridge	4' 8"	Polished Ebony	9,000.
51	5' 1"	Polished Ebony	12,500.
Hampton	5' 5"	Ebony	23,600.
Hampton	5' 5"	Cherry	23,600.
Hampton	5' 5"	Walnut	23,600.
Hampton	5' 5"	Inlaid Cherry	28,000.
Hampton	5' 5"	Inlaid Walnut	28,000.
Prelude	5' 6"	Polished Ebony	9,800.
Cambridge	5' 6"	Polished Ebony	11,000.
Cambridge	5' 6"	Polished Teak Inlay	11,590.
Cambridge	5' 6"	Mahogany Inlay	11,590.

*For explanation of terms and prices, please see pages 45–50.

Strauss

Verticals

Model	Size	Style and Finish	Price*
UP-108	42"	Continental Polished Ebony	2,518.
UP-108	42"	Continental Polished Mahogany	2,518.
UP-108	42"	Continental Polished Walnut	2,518.
UP-108	42"	*Continental Polished White*	2,623.
UP-110	43"	Continental Polished Ebony	2,625.
UP-110	43"	Continental Polished Mahogany	2,625.
UP-110	43"	Continental Polished Walnut	2,625.
UP-110	43"	*Continental Polished White*	2,728.
UP-117C	46"	Chippendale Polished Ebony	2,728.
UP-117C	46"	Chippendale Polished Mahogany	2,728.
UP-117C	46"	Chippendale Polished Walnut	2,728.
UP-117C	46"	*Chippendale Polished White*	2,833.
UP-117D	46"	Polished Ebony	2,728.
UP-117D	46"	Polished Mahogany	2,728.
UP-117D	46"	Polished Walnut	2,728.
UP-117D	46"	*Polished White*	2,833.
UP-117S	46"	Oak	2,878.
UP-117S	46"	Walnut	2,878.
UP-117S	46"	Chippendale Oak	2,878.
UP-117S	46"	Chippendale Walnut	2,878.
UP-120	48"	Polished Ebony	2,938.
UP-120	48"	Polished Mahogany	2,938.
UP-120	48"	Polished Walnut	2,938.
UP-120	48"	*Polished White*	3,043.
UP-120E	48"	Walnut	3,500.
UP-130	52"	Polished Ebony	3,665.
UP-130	52"	Polished Mahogany	3,665.
UP-130	52"	Polished Walnut	3,665.
UP-130	52"	*Polished White*	3,778.

Grands

Model	Size	Style and Finish	Price*
GP-170	5' 5"	Polished Ebony	8,000.
GP-170	5' 5"	*Polished Mahogany*	8,000.
GP-170	5' 5"	*Polished Walnut*	8,000.
GP-170	5' 5"	*Polished White*	8,000.

Model	Size	Style and Finish	Price*

Walter, Charles R.

Verticals

Model	Size	Style and Finish	Price*
1520	43"	Oak	7,079.
1520	43"	Cherry	7,324.
1520	43"	Walnut	7,354.
1520	43"	Mahogany	7,466.
1520	43"	Riviera Oak	7,058.
1520	43"	Italian Provincial Oak	7,089.
1520	43"	Italian Provincial Walnut	7,354.
1520	43"	French Provincial Oak	7,354.
1520	43"	French Provincial Walnut	7,568.
1520	43"	French Provincial Cherry	7,568.
1520	43"	Country Classic Oak	7,120.
1520	43"	Country Classic Cherry	7,262.
1520	43"	Queen Anne Oak	7,640.
1520	43"	Queen Anne Cherry	7,640.
1520	43"	Queen Anne Mahogany	7,640.
1500	45"	Ebony	6,885.
1500	45"	Polished Ebony	7,222.
1500	45"	Oak	6,610.
1500	45"	Walnut	6,824.
1500	45"	Mahogany	6,997.
1500	45"	Cherry	6,997.
1500	45"	Gothic Oak	7,018.

Grands

Model	Size	Style and Finish	Price*
W-190	6' 4"	Ebony	30,694.
W-190	6' 4"	Semi-Polished Ebony	31,312.
W-190	6' 4"	Mahogany	31,930.
W-190	6' 4"	Semi-Polished Mahogany	32,342.
W-190	6' 4"	Walnut	31,930.
W-190	6' 4"	Semi-Polished Walnut	32,342.
W-190	6' 4"	Cherry	31,930.
W-190	6' 4"	Semi-Polished Cherry	32,342.
W-190	6' 4"	Oak	29,870.
W-190	6' 4"	Chippendale Mahogany	32,960
W-190	6' 4"	Chippendale Semi-Polished Mahogany	33,372.
W-190	6' 4"	Chippendale Cherry	32,960.
W-190	6' 4"	Chippendale Semi-Polished Cherry	33,372.

*For explanation of terms and prices, please see pages 45–50.

Model	Size	Style and Finish	Price*

Weber

Model numbers with two digits designate models from Korea, with three digits, from China.

Verticals

Model	Size	Style and Finish	Price*
W-109	43"	Continental Polished Ebony	3,380.
W-109	43"	Continental Polished Walnut	3,500.
W-109	43"	Continental Polished Mahogany	3,500.
W-109	43"	Continental Polished White	3,440.
W-109	43"	Continental Polished Ivory	3,440.
W-41A	43"	Continental Polished Ebony	4,200.
W-41A	43"	Continental Walnut	4,460.
W-41A	43"	Continental Polished Walnut	4,460.
W-41A	43"	Continental Polished Mahogany	4,460.
W-41A	43"	Continental Polished Brown Mahogany	4,460.
W-41A	43"	Continental Polished White	4,240.
W-41A	43"	Continental Polished Ivory	4,240.
WF-41	43"	Cherry	4,600.
WF-41	43"	Mediterranean Oak	4,700.
WF-41	43"	French Provincial Cherry	4,700.
WF-108	43-1/2"	French Cherry	3,900.
WF-108	43-1/2"	Mahogany	3,900.
WF-108	43-1/2"	Italian Walnut	3,900.
WF-108	43-1/2"	Mediterranean Oak	3,900.
WF-108	43-1/2"	Queen Anne Cherry	3,900.
WFX-43	43-1/2"	French Cherry	5,120.
WFD-44	44-1/2"	Mahogany	5,500.
WFD-44	44-1/2"	Oak	5,500.
WFD-44	44-1/2"	French Provincial Cherry	5,500.
W-45C	45"	Chippendale Polished Mahogany	5,780.
WC-46	46"	Continental Polished Ebony	5,180.
WC-46	46"	Continental Polished Mahogany	5,320.
WC-46	46"	Continental Polished Walnut	5,320.
WS-46	46"	American Oak	5,180.
WS-46	46"	American Walnut	5,180.
W-121	48"	Polished Ebony	4,460.
W-121	48"	Polished Mahogany	4,580.
W-121	48"	Polished Walnut	4,580.

Model	Size	Style and Finish	Price*
W-48	48"	Ebony	5,800.
W-48	48"	Polished Ebony	5,800.
W-48	48"	Walnut	6,060.
W-48	48"	Polished Walnut	6,060.
W-48	48"	Polished Mahogany	6,060.
W-48	48"	Polished Brown Mahogany	6,060.
W-131	52"	Polished Ebony	4,880.
W-53	52"	Polished Ebony	6,600.
W-53	52"	Polished Mahogany	6,880.

Grands

Model	Size	Style and Finish	Price*
WG-150	4' 11-1/2"	Polished Ebony	9,500.
WG-50	4' 11-1/2"	Ebony	11,180.
WG-50	4' 11-1/2"	Polished Ebony	11,180.
WG-50	4' 11-1/2"	Walnut	11,920.
WG-50	4' 11-1/2"	Polished Walnut	11,920.
WG-50	4' 11-1/2"	Polished Mahogany	11,920.
WG-50	4' 11-1/2"	Polished Brown Mahogany	11,920.
WG-50	4' 11-1/2"	Cherry	11,920.
WG-50	4' 11-1/2"	Polished White	11,580.
WG-50	4' 11-1/2"	Polished Ivory	11,580.
WG-50	4' 11-1/2"	Queen Anne Polished Ebony	13,120.
WG-50	4' 11-1/2"	Queen Anne Polished Mahogany	13,620.
WG-50	4' 11-1/2"	Queen Anne Polished Brown Mahogany	13,620.
WG-50	4' 11-1/2"	Queen Anne Cherry	13,620.
WG-50	4' 11-1/2"	Queen Anne Oak	13,620.
WG-50	4' 11-1/2"	Queen Anne Polished White	13,420.
WG-50	4' 11-1/2"	Queen Anne Polished Ivory	13,420.
WG-51	5' 1"	Ebony	12,200.
WG-51	5' 1"	Polished Ebony	12,200.
WG-51	5' 1"	Walnut	12,740.
WG-51	5' 1"	Polished Walnut	12,740.
WG-51	5' 1"	Polished Mahogany	12,740.
WG-51	5' 1"	Polished Brown Mahogany	12,740.
WG-51	5' 1"	Cherry	12,740.
WG-51	5' 1"	Polished White	12,640.
WG-51	5' 1"	Polished Ivory	12,640.
WG-57	5' 7"	Ebony	14,260.

*For explanation of terms and prices, please see pages 45–50.

Model	Size	Style and Finish	Price*

Weber (continued)

Model	Size	Style and Finish	Price*
WG-57	5' 7"	Polished Ebony	14,260.
WG-57	5' 7"	Walnut	14,860.
WG-57	5' 7"	Polished Walnut	14,860.
WG-57	5' 7"	Polished Mahogany	14,860.
WG-57	5' 7"	Polished Brown Mahogany	14,860.
WG-57	5' 7"	Cherry	14,860.
WG-57	5' 7"	Polished White	14,660.
WG-57	5' 7"	Polished Ivory	14,660.
WG-60	6' 1"	Ebony	15,160.
WG-60	6' 1"	Polished Ebony	15,160.
WG-60	6' 1"	Polished Ivory	15,760.
WG-70	7'	Ebony	23,500.
WG-70	7'	Polished Ebony	23,500.
WG-90	9'	Ebony	46,760.
WG-90	9'	Polished Ebony	46,760.

Weinbach

Note: Prices below do not include bench. Add from $220 to $630 (most are under $400), depending on choice of bench.

Verticals

Model	Size	Style and Finish	Price*
114-I	45"	Demi-Chippendale Polished Walnut	5,500.
114-I	45"	Demi-Chippendale Pol.Flame Mahogany	5,500.
114-IC	45"	Chippendale Polished Walnut	5,780.
114-IC	45"	Chippendale Polished Flame Mahogany	5,780.
114-II	45"	Polished Ebony	4,780.
114-II	45"	Polished Walnut	4,780.
114-II	45"	Polished Flame Mahogany	4,780.
114-IV	45"	Polished Ebony	5,180.
114-IV	45"	Polished Walnut	5,180.
114-IV	45"	Polished Flame Mahogany	5,180.
124-II	50"	Polished Ebony	6,180.
124-II	50"	Polished Walnut	6,180.
124-II	50"	Polished Flame Mahogany	6,180.

Model	Size	Style and Finish	Price*
Grands			
155	5' 3"	Polished Ebony	16,380.
155	5' 3"	Polished Walnut	16,380.
155	5' 3"	Polished Flame Mahogany	16,380.
170	5' 8"	Polished Ebony	17,580.
170	5' 8"	Polished Walnut	17,580.
170	5' 8"	Polished Flame Mahogany	17,580.
192	6' 4"	Polished Ebony	20,180.
192	6' 4"	Polished Walnut	20,180.
192	6' 4"	Polished Flame Mahogany	20,180.

Welmar

Prices are FOB England and do not include duty, freight, and other costs of importing. Oak, ash, and cherry are available at the same price as mahogany. Polished white is available at the same price as polished ebony.

Model	Size	Style and Finish	Price*
Verticals			
112	44"	Polished Ebony	11,900.
112	44"	Mahogany	10,420.
112	44"	Polished Mahogany	11,900.
112	44"	Walnut	10,420.
112	44"	Polished Walnut	11,900.
112	44"	Teak	10,420.
112 School	44"	Mahogany	10,980.
112 School	44"	Oak	10,980.
114	44"	Polished Ebony	12,120.
114	44"	Mahogany	10,800.
114	44"	Polished Mahogany	12,120.
114	44"	Walnut	10,800.
114	44"	Polished Walnut	12,120.
114	44"	Teak	10,800.
114 Regency	44"	Mahogany	11,460.
114 Regency	44"	Polished Mahogany	12,720.
118	46"	Polished Ebony	13,020.
118	46"	Mahogany	11,540.
118	46"	Polished Mahogany	13,020.
118	46"	Walnut	11,540.
118	46"	Polished Walnut	13,020.

*For explanation of terms and prices, please see pages 45–50.

Model	Size	Style and Finish	Price*
Welmar (continued)			
122	48"	Polished Ebony	13,400.
122	48"	Mahogany	11,920.
122	48"	Polished Mahogany	13,400.
122	48"	Walnut	11,920.
122	48"	Polished Walnut	13,400.
122 School	48"	Mahogany	12,020.
122 School	48"	Oak	12,020.
126	50"	Polished Ebony	13,960.
126	50"	Mahogany	12,780.
126	50"	Polished Mahogany	13,960.
126	50"	Walnut	12,780.
126	50"	Polished Walnut	13,960.
Grands			
183	6'	Polished Ebony	36,620.

Westbrook

Model	Size	Style and Finish	Price*
Verticals			
CFR006	43"	Country French Walnut	2,790.
CFR006	43"	Country French Oak	2,790.
CFR006	43"	Country French Cherry	2,830.
TR006	43"	Walnut	2,790.
TR006	43"	Oak	2,790.
TR006	43"	Cherry	2,830.
MP005	43"	Polished Ebony	2,590.
MP005	43"	Polished Walnut	2,590.
MP005	43"	Polished Mahogany	2,590.
MP005	43"	Polished Cherry	2,590.
MP005	43"	Polished White	2,790.
MP012	48"	Polished Ebony	2,990.
MP012	48"	Polished Walnut	2,990.
MP012	48"	Polished Mahogany	2,990.
MP012	48"	Polished Cherry	2,990.

Model	Size	Style and Finish	Price*

Woodchester

Also available by special order in Teak, Rosewood, Cherry, and Oak, and with Marquetry, if not already indicated.

Verticals

Model	Size	Style and Finish	Price
Arlingham	44"	Tudor Mahogany with Inlays	6,920.
Arlingham	44"	Tudor Polished Mahogany with Inlays	7,980.
Arlingham	44"	Tudor Polished Burled Walnut w/Inlays	8,280.
Arlingham	44"	Tudor Continental Teak w/Inlays	7,360.
Concerto	47-1/2"	Mahogany with Inlays	11,480.
Concerto	47-1/2"	Polished Mahogany with Inlays	12,520.
Concerto	47-1/2"	Tudor Polished Mahogany with Inlays	13,200.
Concerto	47-1/2"	Polished Cherry w/Marquetry & Inlays	14,240.
Concerto	47-1/2"	Polished Rosewood with Inlays	13,300.
Burleigh	48"	Mahogany with Marquetry	10,920.
Burleigh	48"	Polished Mahogany with Marquetry	11,980.
Burleigh	48"	Polished Walnut with Marquetry	12,160.

Wurlitzer

Verticals

Model	Size	Style and Finish	Price
1175A	37"	Country Oak	3,100.
1176N	37"	Queen Anne Cherry	3,100.
2270A	42"	Ribbon-Striped Mahogany	3,590.
2275B	42"	Country Oak	3,590.
2276B	42"	Queen Anne Cherry	3,590.
WP50	42"	Continental Polished Ebony	2,590.
WP50	42"	Continental Polished Cherry	2,590.

Grands

Model	Size	Style and Finish	Price
C143	4' 7"	Ebony	9,180.
C143	4' 7"	Polished Ebony	9,180.
C143	4' 7"	Polished Mahogany	9,460.
C143	4' 7"	Polished Oak	9,460.
C143	4' 7"	Polished White	9,180.
C153	5' 1"	Ebony	10,620.
C153	5' 1"	Polished Ebony	10,620.
C153	5' 1"	Polished Mahogany	11,000.
C153	5' 1"	Walnut	11,000.

*For explanation of terms and prices, please see pages 45–50.

Model	Size	Style and Finish	Price*

Wurlitzer (continued)

Model	Size	Style and Finish	Price*
C153	5' 1"	Oak	11,000.
C153	5' 1"	Polished Ivory	10,620.
C153QA	5' 1"	Queen Anne Polished Mahogany	12,820.
C153QA	5' 1"	Queen Anne Oak	12,820.
C153QA	5' 1"	Queen Anne Cherry	12,820.
C173	5' 8"	Ebony	11,720.
C173	5' 8"	Polished Ebony	11,720.
C173	5' 8"	Polished Mahogany	12,080.
C173	5' 8"	Polished White	11,720.

Yamaha

Verticals

Model	Size	Style and Finish	Price*
M1F	44"	Continental Ebony	5,390.
M1F	44"	Continental Polished Ebony	5,490.
M1F	44"	Continental American Walnut	5,590.
M1F	44"	Continental Polished Mahogany	6,790.
M1F	44"	Continental Polished White	6,690.
M450	44"	American Oak	3,590.
M450	44"	Cherry	3,590.
M500	44"	Cottage Cherry	4,590.
M500	44"	Country Manor Light Oak	5,890.
M500	44"	Country Villa White Oak	6,090.
M500	44"	Florentine Light Oak	4,590.
M500	44"	Georgian Mahogany	5,490.
M500	44"	Hancock Brown Cherry	3,990.
M500	44"	Milano Dark Oak	4,590.
M500	44"	Parisian Cherry	5,690.
M500	44"	Queen Anne Cherry	4,790.
M500	44"	Queen Anne Dark Cherry	4,790.
M500	44"	Sheraton Mahogany	3,990.
P22	45"	American Walnut	4,790.
P22	45"	Black Oak	4,790.
P22	45"	Dark Oak	4,790.
P22	45"	Light Oak	4,790.
P2F	45"	Continental Polished Ebony	5,890.
P2F	45"	Continental Polished Mahogany	6,990.

Model	Size	Style and Finish	Price*
T116	45"	Polished Ebony	4,990.
T116	45"	Polished Mahogany	5,890.
U1	48"	Ebony	7,190.
U1	48"	Polished Ebony	7,290.
U1	48"	American Walnut	7,590.
U1	48"	Polished American Walnut	8,190.
U1	48"	Polished Mahogany	8,190.
U1	48"	Polished White	8,390.
T121	48"	Polished Ebony	5,990.
U3	52"	Polished Ebony	9,690.
U3	52"	Polished Mahogany	10,790.
U5	52"	Polished Ebony	11,390.

Disklavier Verticals

Model	Size	Style and Finish	Price*
MX80A	44"	Continental Polished Ebony	9,666.
MX80A	44"	Continental American Walnut	9,590.
MX80A	44"	Continental Polished Mahogany	10,790.
MX80A	44"	Continental Polished White	10,690.
MX85	44"	Country Manor Light Oak	10,190.
MX85	44"	Country Villa White Oak	10,390.
MX85	44"	Georgian Mahogany	9,790.
MX85	44"	Parisian Cherry	9,990.
MX85	44"	Queen Anne Cherry	9,090.
MX85	44"	Queen Anne Dark Cherry	9,090.
MX88	45"	American Walnut	9,486.
MX88	45"	Dark Oak	9,486.
MX88	45"	Black Oak	9,486.
MX88	45"	Light Oak	9,486.
MX1	48"	Polished Ebony	13,090.
MX1	48"	American Walnut	13,418.
MX1	48"	Polished Mahogany	13,990.
MX1	48"	Polished White	13,280.

MIDIPiano (Silent) Verticals

Model	Size	Style and Finish	Price*
MP50	44"	Cottage Cherry	6,790.
MP50	44"	Country Manor Light Oak	8,258.
MP50	44"	Country Villa White Oak	8,470.
MP50	44"	Florentine Light Oak	6,790.

*For explanation of terms and prices, please see pages 45–50.

Model	Size	Style and Finish	Price*
Yamaha (continued)			
MP50	44"	Georgian Mahogany	7,834.
MP50	44"	Hancock Brown Cherry	6,590.
MP50	44"	Milano Dark Oak	6,790.
MP50	44"	Parisian Cherry	8,046.
MP50	44"	Queen Anne Cherry	6,990.
MP50	44"	Queen Anne Dark Cherry	6,990.
MP50	44"	Sheraton Mahogany	6,590.
MP51	44"	Continental Polished Ebony	7,690.
MP22	45"	American Walnut	7,190.
MP1	48"	Polished Ebony	9,424.
Disklavier Verticals with Silent Feature			
MPX1	48"	Polished Ebony	14,150.
MPX1	48"	American Walnut	14,684.
MPX1	48"	*Polished Mahogany*	15,290.
MPX1	48"	Polished White	14,506.
Grands			
GA1	4' 11"	Polished Ebony	10,390.
GP1	5' 3"	Polished Ebony	11,990.
GH1B	5' 3"	Ebony	12,990.
GH1B	5' 3"	Polished Ebony	13,290.
GH1B	5' 3"	American Walnut	14,790.
GH1B	5' 3"	Polished American Walnut	14,790.
GH1B	5' 3"	Polished Mahogany	14,790.
GH1B	5' 3"	Polished Ivory	14,790.
GH1B	5' 3"	Polished White	14,390.
GH1FP	5' 3"	French Provincial Cherry	17,990.
C1	5' 3"	Ebony	16,790.
C1	5' 3"	Polished Ebony	17,090.
C1	5' 3"	American Walnut	19,290.
C1	5' 3"	Polished Mahogany	19,990.
C1	5' 3"	Polished White	19,290.
C2	5' 8"	Ebony	19,090.
C2	5' 8"	Polished Ebony	19,390.
C2	5' 8"	American Walnut	21,990.
C2	5' 8"	Polished American Walnut	22,690.

Model	Size	Style and Finish	Price*
C2	5' 8"	Polished Mahogany	21,990.
C2	5' 8"	Light American Oak	21,990.
C2	5' 8"	Polished White	20,790.
C3	6' 1"	Ebony	26,190.
C3	6' 1"	Polished Ebony	26,390.
C3	6' 1"	American Walnut	28,990.
C3	6' 1"	Polished Mahogany	29,390.
S4	6' 3"	Polished Ebony	47,390.
C5	6' 7"	Ebony	28,290.
C5	6' 7"	Polished Ebony	28,490.
C6	6' 11"	Ebony	31,390.
C6	6' 11"	Polished Ebony	31,590.
S6	6' 11"	Polished Ebony	53,590.
C7	7' 6"	Ebony	35,790.
C7	7' 6"	Polished Ebony	35,990.
CFIIIS	9'	Polished Ebony	97,990.

Disklavier Grands

Model	Size	Style and Finish	Price*
DGA1XG	4' 11"	Polished Ebony (playback only)	18,990.
DGP1XG	5' 3"	Polished Ebony (playback only)	19,738.
DGP1 IIXG	5' 3"	Polished Ebony	23,190.
DGH1BXG	5' 3"	Polished Ebony (playback only)	21,030.
DGH1BIIXG	5' 3"	*Ebony*	24,190.
DGH1BIIXG	5' 3"	Polished Ebony	24,490.
DGH1BIIXG	5' 3"	American Walnut	25,990.
DGH1BIIXG	5' 3"	*Polished American Walnut*	25,990.
DGH1BIIXG	5' 3"	*Polished Mahogany*	25,990.
DGH1BIIXG	5' 3"	*Polished Ivory*	25,990.
DGH1BIIXG	5' 3"	Polished White	25,590.
DC1 IIXG	5' 3"	*Ebony*	27,990.
DC1 IIXG	5' 3"	Polished Ebony	28,290.
DC1 IIXG	5' 3"	*Polished American Walnut*	31,990.
DC1 IIXG	5' 3"	*Polished Mahogany*	31,190.
DC1 IIXG	5' 3"	*Polished Ivory*	30,990.
DC1 IIXG	5' 3"	*Polished White*	30,490.
DC2 IIXG	5' 8"	*Ebony*	30,290.
DC2 IIXG	5' 8"	Polished Ebony	30,590.

*For explanation of terms and prices, please see pages 45–50.

Model	Size	Style and Finish	Price*
Yamaha (continued)			
DC2 IIXG	5' 8"	American Walnut	33,190.
DC2 IIXG	5' 8"	*Polished American Walnut*	33,890.
DC2 IIXG	5' 8"	*Polished Mahogany*	33,190.
DC2 IIXG	5' 8"	Polished White	31,990.
DC3 IIXG	6' 1"	*Ebony*	37,390.
DC3 IIXG	6' 1"	Polished Ebony	37,590.
DC3 IIXG	6' 1"	American Walnut	40,190.
DC3 IIXG	6' 1"	*Polished Mahogany*	40,590.
DC5 IIXG	6' 7"	Ebony	39,490.
DC5 IIXG	6' 7"	Polished Ebony	39,690.
DC6 IIXG	6' 11"	Ebony	42,590.
DC6 IIXG	6' 11"	Polished Ebony	42,790.
DC7 IIXG	7' 6"	Ebony	46,990.
DC7 IIXG	7' 6"	Polished Ebony	47,190.
MIDIPiano (Silent) Grands			
MPC1	5' 3"	Polished Ebony	21,794.
MPC2	5' 8"	Polished Ebony	24,084.
MPC3	6' 1"	Polished Ebony	31,058.
MPC6	6' 11"	Polished Ebony	36,590.
MPC7	7' 6"	Polished Ebony	40,812.
Disklavier Grands with Silent Feature			
DC1S	5' 3"	Polished Ebony	30,290.
DC2S	5' 8"	Polished Ebony	32,590.
DC3S	6' 1"	Polished Ebony	39,590.
DC3PRO	6' 1"	Polished Ebony	45,380.
DS4PRO	6' 3"	Polished Ebony	67,990.
DC5PRO	6' 7"	Polished Ebony	47,480.
DC6PRO	6' 11"	Polished Ebony	50,580.
DS6PRO	6' 11"	Polished Ebony	74,190.
DC7PRO	7' 6"	Polished Ebony	54,980.
DCFIIISPRO	9'	Polished Ebony	122,590.

Model	Size	Style and Finish	Price*

Young Chang

Verticals

Model	Size	Style and Finish	Price*
E-109	43"	Continental Polished Ebony	2,700.
E-109	43"	Continental Polished Red Mahogany	2,790.
E-109	43"	Continental Polished Brown Mahogany	2,790.
E-109	43"	Continental Polished Ivory	2,700.
E-109	43"	Continental Polished White	2,700.
LC110 AX	43"	Cherry	2,990.
LC110 AX	43"	Walnut	2,990.
PE-102	43"	Continental Polished Ebony	3,190.
PE-102	43"	Continental Polished Walnut	3,790.
PE-102	43"	Continental Polished Red Mahogany	3,590.
PE-102	43"	Continental Polished Brown Mahogany	3,590.
PE-102	43"	Continental Polished Oak	3,790.
PE-102	43"	Continental Polished Ivory	3,390.
PE-102	43"	Continental Polished White	3,390.
U-109C	43"	Queen Anne Polished Ebony	3,990.
U-109C	43"	Queen Anne Polished Walnut	4,300.
U-109C	43"	Queen Anne Polished Red Mahogany	4,500.
AF-108	43-1/2"	Mahogany	3,190.
AF-108	43-1/2"	Italian Provincial Walnut	3,190.
AF-108	43-1/2"	Mediterranean Oak	3,190.
AF-108	43-1/2"	French Provincial Cherry	3,190.
AF-108	43-1/2"	Queen Anne Cherry	3,190.
PF-110	43-1/2"	Mahogany	4,390.
PF-110	43-1/2"	Italian Provincial Walnut	4,190.
PF-110	43-1/2"	Mediterranean Oak	4,790.
PF-110	43-1/2"	French Provincial Cherry	5,190.
PF-110	43-1/2"	Queen Anne Cherry	4,990.
PF-110	43-1/2"	Queen Anne Oak	4,590.
U-116	46-1/2"	Ebony	4,190.
U-116	46-1/2"	Polished Ebony	4,190.
U-116	46-1/2"	American Walnut	4,500.
U-116	46-1/2"	American Oak	4,500.
U-116	46-1/2"	Polished Oak	4,590.
U-116S	46-1/2"	American Walnut (School)	4,390.
U-116S	46-1/2"	American Oak (School)	4,390.

*For explanation of terms and prices, please see pages 45–50.

Model	Size	Style and Finish	Price*
Young Chang (continued)			
F-116	46-1/2"	Mediterranean Oak	5,190.
F-116	46-1/2"	Italian Provincial Walnut	4,990.
F-116	46-1/2"	French Provincial Cherry	5,500.
E-118	47"	Polished Ebony	3,190.
E-118	47"	Polished Red Mahogany	3,300.
E-118	47"	Polished Brown Mahogany	3,300.
E-118S	47"	American Walnut (School)	3,300.
E-118S	47"	American Oak (School)	3,300.
PE-118	47"	Ebony	4,390.
PE-118	47"	Polished Ebony	4,390.
PE-118	47"	Polished Red Mahogany	4,700.
PE-118	47"	Polished Brown Mahogany	4,700.
PE-118	47"	Polished Oak	4,700.
E-121	48"	Ebony	3,390.
E-121	48"	Polished Ebony	3,390.
E-121	48"	Polished Red Mahogany	3,500.
E-121	48"	Polished Brown Mahogany	3,500.
E-121	48"	Walnut	3,500.
E-121	48"	American Oak	3,500.
PE-121	48"	Ebony	4,590.
PE-121	48"	Polished Ebony	4,590.
PE-121	48"	American Walnut	4,790.
PE-121	48"	Walnut	4,900.
PE-121	48"	Polished Walnut	4,900.
PE-121	48"	American Oak	4,790.
PE-121	48"	Polished Oak	4,900.
PE-121	48"	Polished Red Mahogany	4,900.
PE-121	48"	Polished Brown Mahogany	4,900.
E-131	52"	Ebony	3,590.
E-131	52"	Polished Ebony	3,590.
E-131	52"	Polished Red Mahogany	3,700.
E-131	52"	Polished Brown Mahogany	3,700.
U-131	52"	Ebony	5,390.
U-131	52"	Polished Ebony	5,390.
U-131	52"	Walnut	5,790.
U-131	52"	Polished Walnut	5,790.

Model	Size	Style and Finish	Price*
Grands			
TG-150	4' 11-1/2"	Polished Ebony	7,990.
TG-150	4' 11-1/2"	Polished Ivory	7,990.
TG-150	4' 11-1/2"	Polished White	7,990.
G-150	4' 11-1/2"	Ebony	10,190.
G-150	4' 11-1/2"	Polished Ebony	10,190.
G-150	4' 11-1/2"	Polished Red Mahogany	10,790.
G-150	4' 11-1/2"	Polished Brown Mahogany	10,790.
G-150	4' 11-1/2"	Polished Ivory	10,390.
G-150	4' 11-1/2"	Polished White	10,390.
PG-150	4' 11-1/2"	Ebony	11,190.
PG-150	4' 11-1/2"	Polished Ebony	11,190.
PG-150	4' 11-1/2"	Polished Red Mahogany	11,790.
PG-150	4' 11-1/2"	Polished Brown Mahogany	11,790.
PG-150	4' 11-1/2"	Polished Ivory	11,590.
PG-150	4' 11-1/2"	Polished White	11,590.
PG-150D	4' 11-1/2"	Queen Anne Polished Red Mahogany	13,590.
PG-150D	4' 11-1/2"	Queen Anne Cherry	13,590.
PG-150D	4' 11-1/2"	Queen Anne Polished Ivory	13,390.
TG-157	5' 2"	Polished Ebony	8,900.
TG-157	5' 2"	Polished Ivory	8,900.
TG-157	5' 2"	Polished White	8,900.
PG-157	5' 2"	Ebony	12,390.
PG-157	5' 2"	Polished Ebony	12,390.
PG-157	5' 2"	Polished Red Mahogany	12,790.
PG-157	5' 2"	Polished Brown Mahogany	12,790.
PG-157	5' 2"	Polished Ivory	12,590.
PG-157	5' 2"	Polished White	12,590.
PG-157D	5' 2"	Country French Cherry	15,390.
PG-157D	5' 2"	Queen Anne Red Mahogany	15,190.
PG-157D	5' 2"	Queen Anne Cherry	15,390.
PG-157D	5' 2"	Empire Inlaid Polished Brown Mahog.	15,990.
G-175	5' 9"	Ebony	12,790.
G-175	5' 9"	Polished Ebony	12,790.
G-175	5' 9"	Polished Red Mahogany	13,590.
G-175	5' 9"	Polished Brown Mahogany	13,590.
G-175	5' 9"	Polished Ivory	12,990.
G-175	5' 9"	Polished White	12,990.

*For explanation of terms and prices, please see pages 45–50.

Model	Size	Style and Finish	Price*

Young Chang (continued)

Model	Size	Style and Finish	Price*
PG-175	5' 9"	Ebony	14,390.
PG-175	5' 9"	Polished Ebony	14,390.
PG-175	5' 9"	Polished Red Mahogany	15,190.
PG-175	5' 9"	Polished Brown Mahogany	15,190.
PG-175	5' 9"	Oak	15,190.
PG-175D	5' 9"	Empire Inlaid Polished Brown Mahog.	17,590.
PG-185	6' 1"	Ebony	15,990.
PG-185	6' 1"	Polished Ebony	15,990.
PG-185	6' 1"	Polished Walnut	16,790.
PG-185	6' 1"	Polished Red Mahogany	16,790.
PG-185	6' 1"	Polished Brown Mahogany	16,790
PG-185	6' 1"	Polished Ivory	16,590.
PG-208	6' 10"	Ebony	19,990.
PG-208	6' 10"	Polished Ebony	19,990.
PG-213	7'	Ebony	25,190.
PG-213	7'	Polished Ebony	25,190.
G-275	9'	Ebony	59,190.
G-275	9'	Polished Ebony	59,190.